The Adventures
of
Tom McGuire

The Bard of
Typheousina

2nd Edition, vol.1

By Rayner Tapia

Table of Contents

Other Books in series

Multi-Award-Winning books

Morkann's Revenge - vol.2

The Dream Catcher, vol. 3

The Last Enchantment vol.4

Magnificent Reveal vol.5

In memory of my Dad.

Acknowledgments

To my dear family for all your encouragement and sustenance, thank you. To my lovely friends who were always there, for support and love.

For my Mum, for everything you do.

Thank you.

****

What Readers write

5.0 out of 5 stars Tom is an ordinary 10 year old who just happens to be able to travel to other worlds. Tom travels to the land of Oblivionarna where he discovers secrets about his family that have been long hidden. He must also join the battle to save the kingdom from evil! A fantastic sci-fi adventure for all ages! Can't wait to read the rest of the series.
(Amazon review)

5.0 out of 5 stars Such a great book. My son isn't a huge reader but he is enjoying reading this. ***(Amazon review)***

5.0 out of 5 stars It literally was/is a page turner. I've bought the second book too. It would make a great gift. Would love to see this bought to life. Great family saga. (Amazon review)

5.0 out of5 stars I loved this book only because it was interesting and it is a very captivating story that was not too long to read. As I normally dont like reading books this one sunk me right into it with ease. I liked the crossword at the back of the book too. It gave me confidence to read a storybook with enjoyment.

(Facebook review)

Mrs. D rated it was amazing!!
It has really got the imaginative juices
flowing with the imagery to digest.
I have heard this is being made into a movie
too??

5.0 out of 5 stars EPIC!
(Facebook review)

5.0 out of 5 stars Thrilling! *Facebook review*

5.0 out of 5 stars Facebook review
Well done! Thrilling read.

5.0 out of 5 stars -Such great, inspirational talent.

5.0 out of 5 stars -I really enjoyed the
characters and how they developed, the
descriptions are amazing. Admittedly some of
the Latin was a little difficult, but it didn't
take away from the story. It literally was/is a
page turner.
(Amazon review)

5.0 Review from Betsy Gant, for The
Adventures of Tom McGuire.

'These fantastical scenarios are not just
whimsical sci-fi creations but vessels for an
epic drama, where good battles evil. In the
tradition of C.S. Lewis' "Chronicles of
Narnia" and J.R.R. Tolkien's "Lord of the
Rings" series, the fictional universe of "The
Adventures of Tom McGuire" is rich with

Christian symbolism, scripture, and imagery. Dreamy and dramatic, the book's characters may inhabit an alternate world, but in their quest to discern right from wrong, they find real love, are brave in the face of danger and also face every day human struggles. This fast-paced fantasy will appeal to teens and adults alike who enjoy magical adventures. **(Amazon)**

****

Jambalee

Jambalee, the wise one, to guide and assist.

The Tools for the Realm

The Shield of Life, with the Sword of Strength and magic pot of guiding powder

Map of Oblivionarna

The land of Oblivionarna, where light shines, there will always be harmony.

Moraidiya

**Dark demons will only reside where no light will
shine in the land of Moraidiya**

Chapter I

The Beginnings

It was breakfast time in the McGuire household, at number Eight, Beaver Close. The house, was a standard, semi-detached home. It was situated in a quiet Cul-de-sac, at the end of a winding road. The family consisted of Dad, Jed McGuire, Mum, Linda, brothers James and Tom McGuire. Jed worked at Sigma Accounting. He was an accountant. Jed would always leave early in the morning for work. He would always arrive before anyone else would awake. Jed, would leave wearing an immaculate suit, with a vibrant bow tie. He would change his bow ties to a different colour for each day of the week. He thought, a different bow tie with a different colour, would reflect, his different mood for the day in the week. So, if it was. Monday, the colour would be blue, Tuesday it was still blue, but a different shade, on Wednesday, it would be gold and Thursday it was a diamond pattern in red and gold. Friday, it was always green. Jed, along, with his smart attire he would carry his over-filled black briefcase.

The family didn't really do anything out of the ordinary. As a household, they were pretty normal. Some would even suggest, boring.

One would note, they would never, or at least try not to draw attention to themselves. They were the last people you would expect to be involved in anything strange, odd, mystical, magical or different with any weird goings on! It was safe to safe to say, they were the last people who would be involved with anything different. This was, because they just didn't hold such purpose to be tangled in any nonsense!

The children, twelve-year- old James, who had light brown hair, neatly cut behind his ears. He was lean and strong. James, never tolerated nonsense, so he would boss his younger brother around all the time. Although, secretly he loved him, in a strange way. Tom was ten-years-old. He was shorter, sweeter and care-free he would always listen to his big brother, even though sometimes he didn't want to! Tom had brown hair, it was soft and silky, with fringe that would cover his eyes. But he was cute.

Both boys were scoffing and munching on their breakfast, in a rush, to leave for school. There was a lot of commotion.

Jed was very tall; in reality, he could well have been a basketball or a football player, with his strong athletic build.

Jed McGuire, had straight raven hair, which seemed to change shade in the morning light to a sun-kissed fawn. He had sea-blue crystal eyes with long, black long eyelashes. His skin was a sallow olive colour. His entire face was sheer and soft, and only rugged at his razor-sharp jaw line, when he did not shave. His shoulders were angular and strong. It was easy to suggest he was an actor, as he was almost surreal.

He would leave early for work. Jed, would always leave before the boys would go to school. He worked long hours, important hours, all week. Tom and James, didn't really know why he worked so long, but he did. He was an accountant and worked at Sigma Accounting firm. A firm full of numbers, computers and people who didn't really say much. Jed, would be away for a long time at work, sometimes he would long hours away? James and Tom would often wonder would their father return before they were asleep? Linda, Tom's mother, was always stewing, fretting about this and fussing about that. But it was okay, because everyone was happy.

"Hurry up Tom, you always make me late!" moaned James, watching his little brother, munching on his cereal.

James, was a twelve-year-old, smart child. He was in the top set or everything. James would not stand for any 'dilly-dallying' or time-wasting. He would always encourage his brother to do everything correctly and at speed.

"Come along now, are you two ready to go yet?" Linda asked.

"I am!" Tom grumbled, retorting his reply as he munched on his last piece of cereal as quick as he could.

Mum Linda, glared at her young son, Tom endearingly. She watched James, encouraging his brother to speed up and finish his breakfast.

"James, that's enough, leave your brother alone. Tom, try and eat slowly. You'll make yourself sick," Linda insisted, watching Tom, almost choke on his food. She raised her eyebrows, in anguish.

The two boys continued to finish off their final morsels. They were both ready to leave for school. Linda, reminisced about her past life. Her powers, the life of a Princess she had, the tower she lived in, the battles. Which took place

It was Mum, Linda who was always the first-one in the kitchen, that said she was always the first one anywhere. Sometimes even before anyone else would wake-up! Multi-tasking, was what she liked, and did. It was as if by magic Linda would clear-up, tided-up anything and everything in the speed of light. Linda, was thin framed, beautiful, and petite, yet fiercely strong, with a kind smile. She had bright, wide, grey-sky eyes. Linda had autumnal silky hair, which fell to her shoulders.

Linda, had magical powers, but she kept them guarded from her family and private to herself. She knew she must never use her powers on Earth. Certainly, never in front of her family. If she did, the family would discover that Linda was from another world and that she was a Queen and her boys were princes! She would only resort to using her powers when she was sure no one was watching or peeking. Linda, if she had to, would quickly, like a bolt from the blue conduct her method of unique magic.

****

Chapter II

Discovery

"There you go, I've done it!". Linda whispered to herself, hoping no-one was looking or listening. She, turned around only to see Tom, glaring at her, fixed like a statue in wonderment.

Linda gingerly, locked her gaze with Tom. Unsure what she should say, she released a warm smile. "My darling, hurry up now," she said, peering at her young son, while ushering him out. Linda was unsure whether Tom witnessed her magically cleaning up or not. She was always protective over her sons, especially Tom, being the youngest.

After a few stunned moments, Tom, stared at his Mum, this time, he spoke gingerly.

"Wow, Mum, how did you do that?" Asked an astonished Tom, in complete bewilderment.

Linda, stunned, glanced at little Tom. She was caught out in surprise, and that he, DID witness her magic powers. Linda quickly placed her finger firmly on to her pursed lips, "Shoo-ssh- ursh-ussh…". She mimed, hoping that, would be enough for Tom to ignore what he had witnessed. Tom froze in silence. He swallowed, whilst eating his lips. He stared at his Mum. He wanted to question his Mum so much. But he didn't. Linda, locked her eyes with, Tom, in deep concentration. Linda recognised instantly that Tom had seen something peculiar and strange. But they both said nothing to each other. Tom returned a wry smile, as Linda rubbed her hand over his head, flopping his fringe. Tom still wanting his mum to say something but nothing was said. Tom blinked and dipped his head defeated.

Linda, shot her gaze from the corner of her grey eyes, to peer towards Tom as he walked away. She could see, how Tom was awestruck in confusion and lost in thought. Her magic powers, if that's what she did, were over in a flash. Tom had seen them.

Linda of course was in disarray. She pondered, "What if she had to tell her son's of who she really was?"

"What of the turmoil? The fear of what she doomed would happen?" Linda was scared, for the first time, she felt something from the other world had returned? She had never openly used her powers, as matter of fact she had not done so for a long-time. But this time, this time Tom saw, something perhaps he should never have.

Linda always did everything in a regimental manner. So much so, the household, the family felt they could not say anything. The boys had never seen Linda, their Mum, display any of her powers, before so they never discussed it. If Linda did conduct any of her magic, it would always be as a last resort. She was always just so quick as a fox.

"Okay, you better go now, or you'll be late", she said ushering Tom, towards the front door.

Tom, froze, astonished at what his Mum had done and what he had just witnessed.

Tom, feeling, aghast grabbed his school bag still wide-eyed in a confused state. He gazed at his older brother James, for a fleeting second. He was sure his older brother, James did not see what his mother had just done and what she was doing! So, there was no-point in speaking to him. James, was a pre-teenager! He was too studious, worrying about his spots that appeared on his face, and his forthcoming exams.

"Tom, are you leaving? Good, wait for me!" hollered James, oblivious to what had occurred.

Tom waited for James, to throw on his jacket and seize school bag.

"Come-on", he hurried.

Tom still appeared to be in shock.

Linda, saw both boys leave for school. Linda was a hard-working busy Mum, and was happy, in her lot. She never seemed to moan, and if she did her family never saw it.

Mum, Linda was a petite, slim with autumnal-hair. She had small features. She was always smiling and enjoyed being a Mum when she was at home. Although petite she was strong powerful lady, sometimes too strong for her size. There were times, when

Jed, felt their Mum had extra powers! They didn't see anything but it was just her way. Sometimes, Linda would seem invincible. She would volunteer at everywhere. Everywhere at school, the clubs, she even attended the PTA!

Although, Jed would watch Linda in amazement, he would often question, "How do you do that and not get tired?" He would ponder. Of course, there was no answer, except for a smirk and a smile.

This would happen often, leaving Jed, Tom and James always in bewilderment.

Invariably, Linda held the 'magnet of mysteries' close to her heart. She had vowed to her, father, King Cepheus, she would never

release the magnet that she kept firmly closed. The fear of the demon queen, Morkann appearing was frightful. She had many masks and just as much enemies. The fear of her returning to claim with wrath Linda's rightful throne, was too frightening to think about. Linda, knew she would one day have to release her fear to her dear family once and for all. But, although, she the kept the secret of her being Princess now Queen of

Oblivionarna, her sons were growing older and the fear of the demon Princess seeking to oust her and her family was sometimes too much to bear. Her turmoil would never find an opening.

When Tom was born, she realised that she would have to protect Tom from the Demon queen, Morkann. She had vowed to take revenge for the death of her Father and the throne. Linda, knew it would only be a matter of time before the dark forces would reappear. She had to spend some more time with the ones close to her as she had no idea when Morkann would shapeshift and appear to cause havoc.

Linda, never divulged, her anguish or her fear or her past life.

There was so much Linda, could solve, just with a blink. It was stipulated that, Linda, would never return to her land until the demise of demon pretend Queen. But the constraints of the life she had left behind would put her life into danger, and her Father, King Cepheus, on the planets if she persisted in retracing her steps.

Linda and Jed, had everything they ever wished for and more. They were content. Except Linda held a much-guarded secret. Linda, feared it would be discovered now that her sons were older.

Tom was the younger of two boys. Some would say, he was the brother who knew too much too soon. Although he was 10 years old, Tom was still a child. He would always end up following his older brother James everywhere. His older brother, James, was 12 years of age and going on 16. He was a very studious child and loved Maths and History.

James was a very happy-go-lucky person who had lots of friends; he was very relaxed and confident in just about anything he would do. His teachers would recognise this trait and would always take a shine to him.

There was something about James. He had a presence about him and was extremely musical; he played the piano as if he were Beethoven's brother or Mozart's student.

The school, at which both boys attended, would always encourage him. All except Mrs Morecraft. She was not very fond of both James and Tom. There was something, peculiar and very odd about her. Furthermore, she was the most miserable teacher employed at Prosperous High School. Both James and Tom found her attentions somewhat abnormal.

She would always speak to Tom as if he were her long lost son and as if there were no other boys in the class, even though there were 14 other boys in the class, 80 in the year group and 400 in the school.

Mrs Morecraft was a new teacher. She wasn't liked by anyone. She was odd. Her appearance was demonic. She had been teaching history at Prosperous High School for four years. She had a presence about her, was quite authoritarian and not particularly liked by her peers.

The other teachers would avoid her, gawping with her severe green cat's eyes, and leave the room instantly when she would enter. All of her peers, including Mr Jefferson, the headmaster, did not say a word to upset this mysterious and bizarre woman, who just appeared from no-where.

She had a wild mop of wiry, raven-coloured hair, which appeared as if it had just come out of an oven; over-cooked. Her eyes were as green as a meadow where cows could graze.

Her face was a pale shadow of white mist and her cheekbones were trying hard to escape her visage. It was riddled with lines, and no one knew if these lines were of age or lines of disenchantment.

Mrs Morecraft's spindly fingers seemed to increase in size as she wrote or waved her hands in the air at morning registration. Her svelte frame was tall and thin – and when she walked, she almost levitated and glided. Her clothes were drab, she always wore black as if it were the only colour in the spectrum. Her crumpled face and evil sharp eyes, were too malevolent to look at.

Nobody had ever seen her husband, although she was named Mrs Morecraft. Tom, soon realised that there was more to her than he had originally thought. Everyone tended to keep their distance from her. In fact, they would all avoid her like a sour smell! The children would always keep their distance. Tom would always try and steer away from her and try and sit with his friends, who equally kept their distance.

Tom didn't talk to the girls much; he found them somewhat unamusing, what with playing with dolls and talking about the next boy band, which couldn't sing at all. It really was the most uncool thing to talk to a girl! He thought. So, he never did.

However, he did on one occasion manage to say hello to, Alice Butterworth. He thought she was the smartest girl you could ever know, especially when doing your homework in a hurry; she knew just about everything you needed to know, particularly when you were doing Latin or French homework.

The school that Tom attended was called Prosperous High. It was a co-ed school, built around the turn of the century.

There were so many doors, so many windows, large, small with locks and no locks. Narrow corridors, winding walkways all with different floors.

Prosperous High School was an old school built in the early part of the 18th century, which everyone suggested because of its many windows. These were Victorian and had glazed oak sliding sashes with 'antique' glass and glazing bars. The glaze on the bars had become old and turned a pale powder oak colour, flaking and peeing at the bars.

The school had very old creaking doors, cold floors of stone and slate tiles. Although there were lots of large Victorian windows due to the age of the building, everything was always dark – the corridors, the stairs, the classrooms and even the windows themselves. Absolutely everything.

The woodwork appeared like cooked bread and was peppered with woodworm. The door frames were made from old oak, with brass work for the fittings. These were stiff and emulated a ship's iron anchor. They were frozen cold, solid like ice blocks. Some of the brass work was chipped and it would peel or fall off, leaving bits of metal strewn across the floor.

Prosperous High School was named after inspectors had visited and threatened it with closure if the school did not improve.

Therefore, the headmaster, Mr Jefferson, decided that instead of improving he would just rebrand the school.

When this took place some teachers left, others just disappeared, and some simply stayed. Mr Jefferson's plot to try and oust Mrs Morecraft had failed several times. He had tried to get of rid of her and most of the school knew of his ploy; moreover, when some of the teachers were gossiping or leaving, out of all the teachers leaving, she remained.

Faced with the closure of the old school, Mr Jefferson thought that rebranding was all the rage, and of course the whole school, including Tom McGuire and his brother James, were heavily participating in the corridor gossiping. The conversation changed as soon as Mrs Morecraft started teaching at the school, replacing Mr Smith, who was a kind caring individual. Some of the children thought that Mrs Morecraft had driven him out of the school, placing an evil spell upon him.

"Come along children!" bellowed Mrs Morecraft.

Her high-pitched voice seemed to echo, bouncing off one wall to another through the dark concrete corridors of Prosperous High.

All of class, '6M' were lining up to get into Mrs Morecraft's History lesson. There always an awkwardness, for no-one wanted to be the first or last in the queue into her classroom. Mrs Moorcraft was a new teacher. She was odd. Her skin was as pale as a ghost. Her grim face was like that of a carved mask, with chiselled bones protruding though her gaunt face. Her green cat isosceles eyes, were sharp and menacing. Her hands, were spindly, with long thin fingers. Tom was sure, when she raised her hand, her fingers would extend and elongate.

Mrs Morecraft approached the beginning of the line of nervously shuffling children. She looked at the row of children and quickly scanned them with her beady evil eyes. She turned and clasped her spindly fingers, peering down quickly at Tom with her sharp glare. She sneered knowing she had found who she was in search of.

Tom blinked and then quickly looked away, nervously onto the cold slate-tiled floor. He was hoping and praying that Mrs Morecraft would silently not move, not say anything, just unlock the classroom door. He wished she would just go away. Tom just wanted to go through into the classroom and hide in the corner. He felt very uneasy with this new teacher. Mrs Moorcraft, quickly let all the children into the classroom.   He held his breath, counting in his head.

Tom's face cringed and it began to turn red, swelling up like a giant tomato. He could feel his hands become clammy as his books began to slowly slip from his grasp.

"Open the door", prayed Tom silently to himself.

In that nanosecond, Mrs Morecraft had made sure she had informed Tom telepathically of her control over him. She knew she had found who she was in search for. She then released a sarcastic smirk.

The key, once it was put into the lock screeched and clicked, with a clunk and a click, it turned. Tom gawked at every moment the lock clicked open. Mrs Morecraft stretched out her scrawny, emancipated slender fingers. They shook like they were feathers floating. Tom was sure to see more than one hand.

Others thought Mrs Morecraft, who was a Medusa-like figure, had her own intentions to rule the school as well as those in it, including Mr. Jefferson, the headmaster.

This is why it was suggested Mr. Jefferson, the Headmaster, would never dare say anything that

would upset Mrs Morecraft. Her penetrating green cat's eyes were enough to scare even the scariest of monsters. Tom could sense that she was not all as she appeared to be and Mrs Morecraft felt Tom had sensed something strange about her. But she was keen, to confirm, he was the one she was in search for to oust the family and seize the throne for the kingdom.

****

Chapter III

Entering Oblivionarna

The lesson had begun. All the children shuffled noisily to their desks.

"Tom, you WILL sit here," Mrs Morecraft insisted sternly, pointing to an old wooden chair next to her desk.

Tom unhappy with her decision sighed, shuffling and dragging his bag begrudgingly to the desk and chair. The other children looked on in silence, helplessly. After about twenty minutes into the lesson, Tom, was feeling overwhelmed and uneasy from her sly stares. Tom nervously and bravely raised his hand. Quivering, he asked,

"Miss, can I…can I...I?" stammered Tom.

"What is it, Tom?" shrieked Mrs Morecraft. She grimaced. Her mouth stretched wide an evil grin, knowing that Tom wanted to leave her classroom.

"Can I… can I… go to the loo?" said Tom, quivering as he spoke each word.

All the children, gasped a sudden intake of air. They all turned to Tom in unison. The children felt Tom would be in trouble. Their faces, were drowned in shock. Tom swallowed, realising what he had said. Even mentioning to leave the classroom was a great feat!

Mrs Morecraft sneakily glanced at all the other children staring and then quickly locked her stare back down at Tom. She raised her eyes and nodded slowly, "You! Composing herself, she continued, snarling, Don't be long," sneered Mrs Morecraft. Her stern voice, shattering the silence.

She spoke in her malicious manner. All the other children gawked. It was as if she was forced to agree. Tom was able to exit the classroom.

"You can go, she stormed, but come Back!" She barked, twirling her emaciated fingers, over his wrist, then in the air. She then eventually let Tom go, watching his every step.

Tom was used to leaving the classroom. It was just difficult trying to play truant without actually leaving the school. He knew exactly where he was to go. It was a safe place. He knew that his sanctuary was a trusted room, which he always frequented, when he was feeling down. It would be where he would always feel safe. He would always think that anywhere to get away from the clutches of Mrs Morecraft had to be a safe haven.

"She is SO weird", he thought.

Once out of the classroom, Tom began to breathe with relief. What was it that made him feel so insecure?

He quickly, but steadily, walked past the classroom and thought he would stay out for the remaining ten minutes of the History lesson.

As, he walked quietly through the darkened corridor, which seemed to disappear as the midday sun shone through the Victorian windows, his footsteps echoed on the cold slate floor as he headed towards Upper School. He saw James coming out the library and was hoping he would not be seen. Too late! James saw him and ran towards him eagerly. James did not initially see Tom but heard his footsteps bellowing on the floor.

"Tom!" called James surprisingly. "What are you doin' here? You should be in your lesson?"

He queried.

"Crikey! Just come with me," replied Tom, pulling James by the arm and leading him to the boiler room.

"Hey, Tom!"

"What're you doing?" James questioned. He was startled, and then it clicked.

"Oh… Mrs Morecraft!" He said, as he let out a sigh of relief. "Look, just go back, don't worry about it. You can't keep running off like that, plus you are missing all your lessons! Just go back!" James pleaded with his brother. James could see from the look on his brothers' face, that Tom was determined.

James persisted, trying to persuade Tom to return to class, in vain.

"I know SHE is a bit strange, but SHE CAN'T be THAT bad! Can she?"

Tom, ignored his brothers' comments and continued to pull James's arm, goading him towards the boiler room.

James continued with his reasoning for Tom to return to Mrs Morecraft's classroom, but Tom quickened his pace.

"Hey, what's going on? Why are you insistent? Can you just tell me? What's going on? What happened?" pressed a puzzled James.

Tom looked at James and giving him a silent stare, before finally speaking.

"James, you have to be quiet, just quiet. If I tell you, I mean it! You can't tell anyone.

Promise me? Okay, Watch, this James," Tom asserted.

At that point, they approached the boiler room. Tom looked pensively both left and right, licking his lips, he swallowed, worryingly making sure no one was in view of where he was about to go. He turned the handle to the boiler room – click – the door was open.

It was a safe haven for Tom and he knew it, but James did not. James didn't know about the visits Tom had made previously, the characters he had met and befriended. James was not aware of the adventures Tom had got up to. The wild, dangerous escapades he had been through. This was Tom's moment and he would now share it with his angst-ridden brother.

"Come on and keep quiet," whispered Tom to James, ordering an anxious James to walk on.

James warily, listening crept further into the boiler room past a maze of steel pipes that emulated submarine telescopes.

"This is really mad; I can't believe I am following you!" stammered James, looking and turning his head at the maze of pipes and the design of the boiler room.

James's voice seemed to reverberate in the room as he blindly followed his brother.

Finally, Tom approached an old brown-coloured door. It was made of iron, or what looked like iron. It was so old; it was surprising it was still standing.

The door was all rusty. It was evident, the door had changed colour over the years into a burnished brazen bronze, flaking in places from age. James just looked astonished and shocked at where his brother had led him. He was amazed, astounded at this new door, which he had never discovered. This was not surprising as the door was inconspicuous, lurking in the corner.

Tom pushed open the door with all his might and all James could see was pitch dark, blackness, leading to nowhere. It looked like a void. Complete blackness. Tom turned to his brother, eagerly, hoping he had changed his mind.

"You coming?" Tom asked.

"N… n… NO, I don't think so, this is not a good idea!" James stuttered cautiously, "Tom, I don't know about this. I'll just wait here for you here."

"Are you sure?"

"Yes, I will wait here for you. There is no way I AM Going in there! I mean look at it! it's completely a void of nothingness! I can't see anything!" James roared, furious at Tom not being in his classroom and to top it luring him into the Boiler room.

Tom, walked further into the darkness. This was always petrifying; The fear of the unknown.

A puzzled James sat back on a sack of coal, trying to make himself comfortable, he found next to the door. He waited pensively, moaning to himself. He thought about leaving the boiler- room and then how he would very quickly to get back through the boiler room. What would happen should Tom need his help. James was completely quandary. His mind was in a real whirl.

Tom continued to push the door; he tugged and heaved. James just watched curiously, helpless yet wanting to assist, but he was scared. Tom, with one last push, entered the land of Oblivionarna.

Tom didn't know where this land was, except that the further he walked, the further he would encounter tribulations and various episodes of excitement. Each time he would visit a character called Jambalee, who would pop up and guide him through the dense, dark terrain, walking past old trees that would bow to greet him as if they knew their king had returned.

The old trees that fell over arching the pathway into Oblivionarna would glisten in the blue-purple hazy light that engulfed the land. Tom stood still, feeling the cold, still wind falling through the trees leaving angel shadows through the fissure, when suddenly out popped, as expected, Jambalee.

Jambalee was a strange character. He had small, tiny little feet and a protruding stomach that was held in by his tweed-coloured trousers. His green coat, which had a tail, was rather too small for him; there was one button in brown leather holding the entire jacket together. His ears were large and stuck out as if he were trying to catch something.

His eyes were small, round droplets of purple orbs. His hair jutted out like spikes of green blades emulating grass. It exploded out of an old, triangular, pointed conical hat. It could have belonged to a witch? His feet stuck out and flapped in a pair of old unpolished black shoes with a bulbous round toe. His brown coat, was wrapped around his waist.

His feet stuck out and flapped in a pair of old unpolished black shoes with a bulbous round toe.

Although this character was strange, he was a friend to Tom.

"So, you've come back?" questioned Jambalee excitedly.

"Yes, yes I have! Yep, what's happened?" asked Tom. He eagerly, scanned his surroundings.

Tom seemed to know that Oblivionarna had suffered and Typhoeusina was responsible once again.

Oblivionarna was a land of mystery and was covered with a verdant carpet, of tranquil. It's marshes were rich in life. It suffered from various atmospheric weather conditions – fog, mist and ice – along with hazy moonlight and red darkness in crisp, clear, cold nights.

****

Chapter IV

The Oracle at Uroboros

Tom and Jambalee ambled through the marshes, Although, there was silence. Tom began to ask about what Typhoeusina had been up to.

"Typhoeusina, oh, the evil tyrant dragon still wants to reclaim all the land and huts from the U-Targ, Daga and Pastureman and troll folk. Typhoeusina has made many homeless," whimpered a worried Jambalee. He continued,

"The U-Targ were once proud giants who lived peacefully alongside the Daga, Trolls on Sky Mountain until Typhoeusina came along and cruelly began to wipe them out."

Jambalee dipped his head.

They were willowy and loving, with brightly coloured eyes and long, slender fingers just like Tom and his Mum's, which is probably why the U-Targ, Trolls and Daga took to Tom automatically. The U-Targ could read the future and would often visit the Circle of Life. Here they would have to cross a snake, creature. with two cone heads protruding from its slithery, scaly covered skin with dazzling, hypnotic sapphire eyes.

Every day the U-Targ would do this to ask the Oracle of Life, if they would survive another exhausting battle with Typhoeusina. The Dragon was ruthless. Typhoeusina, was a monster dragon with a hundred serpent' heads. All with fiery red eyes and a tremendous voice, which, when roared, shattered the whole of Oblivionarna, causing destruction on a colossal scale.

All who lived in Oblivionarna – the Lupans, Dillyans and the Wish Unicorn – were frightened of Typhoeusina and would never dare raise a whisper to it.

Jambalee led Tom to Grimm's Marsh, where the remaining U-Targ, Daga and Trolls were camped.

'Look!' Jambalee cautiously spoke, pointing to the camps where the now dwarfed, U-Targ were trying to live. These were people who were once giants in stature and in size but had become dwarfed by a horrendous battle with Typhoeusina many moons previously.

Tom peered nervously through the reefs.

"What has he done?" He whispered helplessly to himself. "Typhoeusina, could you not wait?" He muttered, helplessly, to himself.

Tom was angry and looked at Jambalee. Tom's eyes were riddled with emotion and in disarray. The turmoil as to what the U-Targ had been through was too much to bear.

"We have to do something. This can't go on",
he said, his voice shattered in despair.

"I feel so helpless!"

Tom was annoyed, as he frowned in despair.

Jambalee looked at Tom.

"We have to go to Uroboros and ask the
Oracle how to stop this!" insisted Jambalee.

"It is only YOU that can only help us now!
PLEASE!"

Tom realised that Jambalee and the U-Targ
were desperate and that something had to be
done. Although petrified, he agreed to help.
He shook Jambalee's hand and promised he
would be back later.

He was led back through the marshes until he
reached the iron door, but when Tom began

to pull the door, it stayed firmly shut. He suddenly became very clammy and agitated.

"Oh c'mon, open!" he shouted, but the door would not. Tom thought about his brother waiting on the other side and the trouble that he would be in.

Jambalee looked at Tom. "It's not going to open; YOU HAVE TO HELP US!" He pleaded. His little droplet eyes fell in a pitiful manner, his brow frowned and Jambalee became teary-eyed and sad.

A reluctant Tom followed him back through the marshes.

"We had better go to the Oracle at Uroboros, then," he said. His voice now rising in anguish.

Once they arrived at Grimm's Marsh camp, Jambalee, who was an eager little creature, presented Tom with the shield of life. The shield was gold in colour and encrusted with rubies and topaz stones, which were all held in diamonds. It had a distinctive engraving on the top of the shield of a hand holding a seed.

"You will need this," said Jambalee.

Tom held the Shield, it was heavy, examining he questioned Tom

"What is it?"

Giving the Shield of Life to Tom, Jambalee gazed, "This is the Shield of Life, it will help you. It is for those who are worthy. Tom, you are a blessed child of the Oracle and by presenting it to you, I know that you will not falter!"

Taking the shield, Tom dropped his. "Woh, this is heavy! Do I have to carry this then?" he asked, looking at Jambalee.

"Yes, you must," Jambalee nodded. "Help us, please."

Tom was ready and he knew the battle would commence very soon. He was mouth dried up. Goosebumps puckered his arms drops of sweat trickled down his forehead. They fell slowly onto his school jumper. His raced. Hid thoughts darted around in his mind. – He could see his Mum, Mrs Morecraft, Mr Smith, and his brother, James, waiting in the boiler room.

All these emotions were whizzing, wildly around in his head like a washing machine spinning every turmoil he was encountering and was about to stumble upon.

Tom marched very closely to Jambalee – he was petrified. The sky became a dark midnight purple and it was bitterly cold as the grey fog gave way to a sheer sinister wisp of steam. All Tom could see and feel was an eerie silence and a greyish milieu as he whispered, "How far are we now?" Tom asked quivering.

"The Oracle is near and you must be brave," replied an anxious Jambalee, holding Tom's wrist.

The clearing was seen in the distance, the skies seemed to change colour and the mist and fog shadowed a bright red cloud peering through the horizon. The ground was laden with thick green moss hovering over the soil, which allowed drops of white flowers to seep through.

"This is it – Uroboros. We must watch out for the great Dragon," Jambalee announced, with a tinge of fear in his voice. Inside, though, he was anxiously questioning whether Tom would achieve his mission – but then Tom was the saviour. Only Jambalee knew of the powers his mother possessed and how she had been allowed to join the mortal world and achieve her goals.

He also knew that Mrs Morecraft was from Moriadiya and she was better known as Morkann. She wanted revenge for the humiliating defeat of her Father, King Polylectes. It was King Cepheus who had won the battle of Typhoona against Typhoeusina, and Polyectes knew he could never achieve success as long as Lindiarna was alive.

Jambalee knew that Tom was not aware of all the obstacles that would befall him. Lindiarna was the daughter of Cepheus. Who had been a Warrior Lord in the days long before Tom or James were born.

King Cepheus was the only Warrior Lord to have successfully killed a Typhoeusina and had injured the wicked King Polyectes in the Battle of Typhoona.

This was where only one of the serpents was slaughtered by King Cepheus, following a ferocious battle in which King Polyectes was forced to accept defeat. Subsequently, the

U-Targ rejoiced, hailing King Cepheus as their War Lord and when Linda, or Lindiarna, was born, she was blessed by the Oracle so that she would have a long life and that no harm would come to her.

The Dillyans, were female imps. They were short, always smiling with sweet features. Their small red lips and huge black round-coloured eyes like pebbles. Darted quickly and at speed. They had long curly ringlet hair. They were chirpy and the enjoyed celebrating and rejoicing the birth of Lindiarna. They held a banquet and danced to the music played by the Wish Unicorn. It was a merry time and all were jolly and happy.

Lindiarna was a very contented child and it was only Morkann, as well as King Polylectes from the maleovant world of Moraidiya, who did not wish to see her live as happy as she was.

Therefore, King Cepheus and Jambalee decided it would be best if Lindiarna, be set free from life in Oblivionarna and galaxy. No one dared utter a whisper or a word of any disagreement. So, it was decided, to keep Lindiarna safe and protected, she would be sent to the mortal world.

As Tom and Jambalee waded on, a two-headed, mystifying serpent appeared, guarding the entrance to the Oracle. Tom looked on with sheer fright etched upon his face, his eyes stretched open and wide with the shock of what he was about to confront.

Jambalee watched a careful Tom ponder on how he should distract the serpent. As the Serpent of Uroboros slid to and fro, his sapphire eyes dazzled like an ocean wave beating the sea bed, blinding anyone who would dare to look at him.

His thick scaly leather snakeskin rolled like a giant sausage, slamming the ground and causing it to shudder. His heads – of which there were two the size of colossal pumpkins – swiped the ground, hitting everything in their path.

"Give me my shield," demanded a brave Tom to Jambalee.

"Are you sure? This may not be the right time."

"We cannot wait," answered Tom, his eyes fixed on the beast that was swaying in front of him. 'The moment in which he begins to devour himself, I will have to strike. If I don't do it now, it will have to wait until tomorrow… and.

Tom argued and shouted as fast as all the words could be said. Jambalee cautiously handed over the Shield of Life, knowing that this would protect him and allow him to enter the Oracle. Holding the shield, it shimmered and the stones began to lift, but they were not moving – it was like watching a mirage.

"What is happening?" Yelled Tom.

Just then, as he watched the serpent rise and protrude his long, slinky, red tongue aiming to grab Tom, a raging roar bellowed.

Typhoeusina had appeared. Tom fleetingly ducked to avoid the swoop of Typhoeusina, but Typhoeusina had seen Tom and was now in sight of his new prey.

Tom, only had to make one disastrous error. He had to remain focused. The minute he lost concentration, the deadly dragon with a hundred heads, would take one lunge and Tom would be yesterday's thought! Tom shook, he opened his hazel eyes wide, like a raccoon. The Dragon caused a huge deathly shadow, as he moved. Tom gulped in horror. Crippled in fear, goosebumps covered the back on his neck and arms. His hands became hot and clammy his heart began to race. Typheousina spotted Tom. He was like a dot the dragon's lair.

"Watch out!" screamed Jambalee. Typhoeusina threw his body backwards and forwards, trying to catch Tom like a fly.

Typhoeusina's heads swayed, rolled and trundled, back and forth with much menace. – They were so many heads, each with fire-red eyes, oozing anger, glaring, and staring, watching every angle of the Oracle. The dragon. swivelled, causing a humongous shadow to loom. The Dragon rotated its demonic, to gl are at it's next morsel. Some of it's heads fell slamming to the rocky ground. Some of the other heads fell, a couple of times onto the rock, bouncing back as if held on elastic. They hit with a roaring boom as each one fell. There did not seem to be any fear in this enormous creature.

The serpent, Typheousina of the Oracle had departed; sliding away in haste. It was obvious no creature remained. They were all too scared to stay and oppose the great Typhoeusina.

Jambalee, was horrified. He had not seen, the full wrath of the deadly Dragon. Jambalee, was disappointed that he could not help, but also that the Shield of Life, had been given and although, it was used, Jambalee did not know how long Tom could sustain its strength.

Tom, not knowing what to do dived underneath Typhoeusina's torso so that he would not be seen by the creature's heads. Typhoeusina rolled it's dazzling evil eyes and pierced the tor in search for his prey.

Typhoeusina looked everywhere and spotted a trembling Jambalee in the corner. He was trying to hide himself, moving very slowly He etched backwards slipping into the marsh undergrowth. It rumbled and squished under his foot.

Jambalee entered an abyss, hoping he would not be seen. He couldn't call out for Tom, as his life would be put into jeopardy and Jambalee knew this.

The tension was excruciating and no one could imagine what the next step would bring.

A solider, from the land of Oblivionarna.

****

Chapter IV

Entering the Circle of Life

The enormous colossal monster serpent, with it's hundred heads. The colour of orange and red, of the colossal fire breathing dragon, was able to burn the ground, leaving shards of black ash everywhere. His heads were heavy, long and thick, covered in barbed, jagged spikes. Each-head swayed and rolled, smashing to the ground, with a booming bang they would slam. They were scary, and

scaley, fearsome and proud! The humongous
lizard-like creature with a long pointed jagged
barbed tail ruled with brutal might. It would
lunge forward breathing fire. It's isosceles
triangular pointing downward eyes, scanned
for its very next morsel. The serpent's scaly
heads with it's enraged eyes would fire it's
wrath to control with ferocious fury. It
paraded the tor, slamming the ground to scare
all around. It ruled with such a brutal might.
Proudly, swaying the with a hundred large
scaled heads. This creature of demonic level
and obtrude fiery dazzling topaz eyes
transfixed like a pelican crossing lamp. His
devilish fire tongue, flickering flames of
sulphur air, seemed to engulf the entire

surrounding like a volcano that had just erupted.

The only difference was that Typhoeusina was able to consume a whole dragon in one gulp! Tom was petrified. Quivering, he locked his gaze and froze. He had never witnessed anything like this even on the telly! He somehow found himself hiding, for life cautiously under Typhoeusina's body. He wondered how long he would be able to sustain his position. This monster dragon was fierce. If Typhoeusina, the deadly dragon, moved, just once, just a millimetre, it would cause Tom to be squashed in the foul stench and weight of the monster's underbelly. Jambalee, peeking out from behind a thick protrusion of marsh reeds, had to do something.

Tom was paralysed, crippled in fear to the spot, where he stood. He was stuck solid under, the deadly dragon Typhoeusina's torso. His palms became sticky, and sweaty. The Shield of Life, slipped from his grasp.

"Crikey, no, no!" He mumbled, closing his yes in

Tom really wanted to scream and run, but his fear became tangible, like a living force that crept over him. He was immobilised. His fear had taken hold. He was just left with his mouth open.

The bejewelled shield was trapped and shimmered in the light as Tom tried desperately and discreetly to pull it towards him. He was tiring and his limbs became sore. They were aching in dull pain, the pain clutched onto his little limbs.

Tom became sad, no-one was there. Jambalee was not to be seen and he felt left all alone.

He was frightened and feeling resigned to his final fate. Tom, glanced around, trying to peek out from under the dragon's torso. Tom, closed his eyes, in despair, as he continued to lie under the thick foul stench of Typhoeusina torso.

Daylight soon gave way to darkness and the sky turned a deep purple. The stars were crisp and twinkling, sparkling like Christmas lights.

Tom, again tried to look around to see if Jambalee had arrived to rescue him. But he was no-where to be seen. Tom wonder where Jambalee had got to, as it felt like he had been stuck in the same position for hours.

'Crikey! Doesn't this monster sleep?' Tom moaned to himself. Suddenly, Jambalee emerged near to Tom.

Tom beamed, but was still unable to move.

"Ssh, shuhsssh..." Jambalee whispered. He was dancing with death, and Tom watched very carefully, peeking through any small space he could find.

Jambalee hopped around to see where Tom was positioned. He very quietly hovered over to Typhoeusina's torso, once he had spotted Tom stuck. He placed his tiny finger to his mouth, informing Tom that he would be saved, but he would have to be very, very quiet.

Looking straight at Tom, Jambalee ushered him to grab hold of a long pole, which he would pass through to him. Tom, dragged himself in position, ready to grab the pole. Jambalee was desperately tried to push through the long pole under the evil serpent's torso.

"I am going to push, this through to you now", Jambalee said, proudly holding the pole. "You must take hold of it Sire, Tom," he whispered, animating with hands of actions. Jambalee started pushing through a long pole, towards Tom.

The wrath of Typheousina.

"When I push it towards you, just hold on tight, pull it, and run."

Tom nodded, his eyes, locked wide open. He was bewildered and surprised at what Jambalee was about to do.

He watched, and waited patiently for the sign. Tom's heart began to pulse faster. The hairs on the back of his neck shot out. His heart raced like a hare on its last race. His veins protruded on his hands. A cold wave embalmed him as the hairs rose on the back of his neck and his mouth ran dry. Sweat droplets glistened over his forehead.

Tom, pensively the Dragon stir. His eyes wide open, like saucers.

Suddenly the serpent began to stir and both Jambalee and Tom stood still. They were crippled in fear, like statues. After a few minutes, which felt too long. Jambalee, levitated away towards where Tom was hiding. Tom began to perspire; he could feel heat all around him. His mouth suddenly became dry, panicking, he gazed everywhere. Terrified, he wondered where, Jambalee had got too.

Suddenly Jambalee shot a shaft very quickly through the reefs towards Typhoeusina's under belly, Tom could barely see remnants of the long pole dangling towards him.

It was a death-defying act, for both Tom and Jambalee. They gasped in baited breath in the horror at the size of the colossal creature. One move and both would dead and eaten alive!

"Now!" Jambalee roared. "Tom, now! Tom! Seize it! Now, Tom! Tom! GRIP IT, GRAB

THE SHAFT TOM! GRAB HOLD OF IT, TOM! THE POLE QUICKLY, NOW!". Jambalee shrieked with tense terror in his voice.

Tom frantically chased the pole, as Jambalee pushed it through under the huge torso of the Dragon. Tom frantically tried to take hold of the pole; but his hands seemed to dance around as he struggled to grab onto it. Tom knew that his life would depend upon it. He peeked through any small space he could. Tom, knew in a quick moment, that if he had any chance of escaping. He had to grab hold of the pole and hold it tightly! Once he caught the pole, he held onto it firmly. His hands firmly clasped around the shaft. Tom, now had one side of the long pole. Jambalee swung the pole onto the other side and under Typhoeusina's torso. The dragon roared a thunderous roar. Giving a ferocious boom, across the land where he sat. Tom, saw the pole slide through under the Dragon's torso towards him. Tom, had lost the ability to scream. His fear had snatched at his voice. His face devoid of any emotion, except he wanted to live and escape! He was now holding onto the long shaft, for dear life. Jambalee, had risked his and Tom's life to push the shaft inconspicuously towards him. It was a miraculous and brave endeavour.

Typheousina, confronts Tom and Jambalee

Typheousina, the deadly dragon, unleashes it's rage, as Tom watches in disbelief.

"Crumbs, I don't know why this is happening? What is going on?" He questioned. Tom was scared stiff. He knew that it was only his inner power that was now keeping him going.

Typhoeusina's heads began to gently sway. They picked up momentum, lolling from side to side, falling everywhere, crashing and banging. Unexpectedly, one of its heads fell slamming to the ground with a booming boom.

The monster dragon, let out a tumultuous groan, raging in deafening anger to whoever was near to him. It reverberated causing nearby rocks to fall into the atmosphere. Jambalee had to continue to help Tom to get away. Tom with one sudden jolt, squirmed out.

Tom was finally out. He ran away. He just ran, anywhere, somewhere, as fast as he could, – just running. The marshes crackled under his feet. He didn't look in which direction he was running – he just ran as fast as his little legs would carry him. /Breathing heavily, petrified, Tom didn't know when to stop, or if he should!

The surrounding marshes tumbled, making a noise reminiscent of a building site; crashing, cranking, bosh... bash...bish, it was riotous and very confusing.

Suddenly, everything shuddered just like an earthquake. The monster turned his dazzling obtruding, ossicles sapphire eyes and gazed at Tom running away and escaping from him.

The dragon, in anger lunged forward, opening his mouth. He had seen his snack escaping. Tom rolled and snuck behind the reeds. The reeds rustled. The dragon emitted an angry jolting noise. It was too late – Typhoeusina had missed his chance. Tom had got away.

Tom and Jambalee had only a few more metres to trudge through the strange land. It was barren, rocky and cold. Before they would enter the Circle of Life at Uroboros. Tom, composed himself, trying to catch his breath after his near-death experience with Typheousina.

"Well, that was a close call?" Suggested, Tom

Jambalee, turned to Tom,

"Yes, you must keep strong! You are a Prince!". Jambalee replied.

Tom, looked up in surprise, but Jambalee continued in his story of the fallen U-Targ, with Daga and Pastureman.

"Well, who are they?" Demanded Tom curiously.

"Yes, dear Tom, let me tell you". Jambalee began to tell the story, "They are the U-Targ. They are creatures who live among flying

Trolls Daga and Pastureman on Sky Mountain, in Oblivionarna near the Mountains of the Moon. They are gentle creatures with a fierce ruler.

They were in a ruthless battle; I mean it was really scary. They fought against the Morkannis,

the evil demonic army of ghouls. The troops, from Oblivionarna, were made-up of Centaurs, and Dillyians. led by Aspero They were brave. They wanted to save the U-Targ from being gobbled up by Typheousina. Aspero is the, brave strong leader of from Oblivionarna.

This is where Lindiarna is from. Remember that name Tom, I shall ask you that again.

They were trying to destroy Typheousina," Jambalee, retold,

"I am still thirsty", Tom whined. Who won the battle? Why did the battle happen?" Tom persisted.

Jambalee, smiling jerked his head towards Tom.

"Tom, you will, be approached, and will be asked, for the U-Targ, to be set free or indeed to ask for Typhoeusina' s wrath to banished".

As they both continued to trek, half stumbling, over the rocky ground, Tom noticed a small creature which could have been dressed up they both pondered silently on what had just happened. Their breath panting like a panther after its prey. Their pulses racing as if they were doing a marathon. Perspiration trickled down onto Tom's face as he wiped if off with his hand.

"That was SO close," Tom said, trying to make sense of escaping from under Typhoeusina's torso.

"The stench of where I was trapped" Tom shook his head.

"We're you scared?" questioned Jambalee.

Tom swallowed.

"I knew you would come!"

So glad when you turned up, when you did!"

"Yes, I was petrified," Tom shook his head, wiping off some grunge from his jacket."

"You are brave, Tom. This is the legacy of King Cepheus and Lindiarna."

"Lindiarna! King Cepheus? Who are those?" He questioned anxiously. I'm so thirsty," Tom moaned, looking at Jambalee.

"Tom, here take this". Jambalee handing him some water from a casket he held in his coat.

"We will be there soon." Jambalee, replied, hoping his reassurance would erase his question.

Jambalee, could see Tom, was feeling deflated and he looked sad as dipped his head in despair.

"You are right. That was a close shave. That multi-headed monster nearly had us

but we managed to get away in the end,' encouraged Jambalee.

"Yes, well you…", replied Tom sharply.

Just before Tom could finish off his sentence, a voice broke in.

"WHO DARE GOES THERE?" it shrieked in a deep, forceful voice. Tom, prettified gazed everywhere. He found himself staring at a demonic oak tree – surprisingly, it was staring straight back at him. The tree was angry. The bark, was solid. proud. It was flaking all over the trunk It's angry face etched on the bark. It had frowning eyes, hollow and dark. The faking trunk, was bunched together to form frowning angry brow! It was well known, on the land, that the tree should not be agitated or disturbed. It was, it would never let anyone pass alive.

To do so would transform the standing angry tree into life. It's ancient, withered branches broke into an army of warriors.

They creaked, and cracked, before an army was revealed.

The Old Oak Tree grumbled and the branches suddenly began to bow. The tree roared, its twigs rustled and its bark rippled as it spoke. The branches stretched and squeaked.

The Old Oak Tree

"You know the rules, Jambalee!" The old tree roared.

"Sir, I had to pass the Serpent of the Oracle and Typhoeusina, with all the…'

"ENOUGH!" Interrupted the Old Oak Tree.

Suddenly, the branches raised their twigs and became rigid and firm, as the tree was standing to attention.

"No, please, your Tree-ness". Tom garbled pleading with the Old Oak Tree, to let them pass.

Tom cautiously barged in, frustrated at the lack of progress Jambalee had made with the Old Oak Tree.

"We are trying to get to the Circle of Life," he said, trying his best to show as much humility as he could.

"We have to ask for help to save the U-Targ, Daga and Pastureman, Trolls on Sky Mountain," he said as he waited for an answer to come forth, Tom snatched a look around him. He saw how the sky had changed its colour to an emerald green and the ground had become suddenly frost-bitten.

"Oh, you are, are you?" groaned the Old Oak Tree. "How dare you defy me – you should know I show no mercy," bellowed the Old Oak Tree.

"Please, we will do anything you say sir, please", pleaded Jambalee.

"Then you must show me how well you can survive here in the, 'Mountains of the Moon'," The Old Oak Tree hollered, in a supercilious tone. The Old Oak finished it's sentence, his voice slowly trailed away and with that, an army of branches, suddenly emerged from the Tree. They were ridged stern and stiff stick like deadly beings. They began to walk, in unison toward Jambalee and Tom.

Tom, and Jambalee, stood still watching, waiting for what the thin lanky branches would do. The menacingly army of branches marched towards them, and they appeared as weird as the elfin lights. They got closer and closer. Tom felt the thin hairs on the back of his neck suddenly shot out, like spokes on a bike wheel.

The ground started to shudder and vibrate. The frozen dew drops started to melt, turning into tiny puddles of blue water as the branches advanced in a sequence, reminiscent of thin stick soldiers marching in a trance.

Tom, was speechless. He stood still watching the weird army stomp on in unison.

Jambalee, worried and horrified, looked at Tom's face, which had melted away with fear.

"Now what?" shouted Tom desperately, waving his arms around as if he were summoning some great God from above.

Jambalee hurriedly grabbed his small purse pouch from over his jacket and ripped off the bottle top. He started throwing white powder onto the branches, his eyes anxious as he threw as much as his little hands could carry.

Jambalee, then took out a small wand from his coat. He waved it high up and down, staring at the marching branches. Jambalee held his wand firmly as purple mist slowly wafted out of the wand.

"Watch, Tom", he said as he slowly backed away, pulling Tom with him by keeping his eyes on the advancing branches still stomping. We must go, quick - run!" He suddenly hollered. "Follow me – quickly!"

As they ran away from the Old Oak, Tom glanced back to catch sight of the result of Jambalee's powder. The branches were one by one were transformed into statues – some still halfway between steps. He turned his attention back to his escape route and ran side by side with Jambalee. The ran through the undergrowth until, breathless and scratched from the thorn bushes that had stood in their way. They came out into a clearing. The army had faded away. Jambalee's powder and wand had worked.

The sky was a still-grey and yet there was a clear white light brightening in the heavens. There were no trees, and the flowers were all a shade of grey.

"Where are we?" a breathless Tom asked, as he stooped to take in some of the cold crisp air into his lungs. Jambalee was walking slightly ahead like a lost child through the desert of grey flowers. "We have now entered the Mountains of the Moon," he answered.

"Wow, this is unbelievable," replied Tom in wonderment.

Smiling to himself, Jambalee knew that the Circle of Life was not far away and he began to relax; his pace slowed yet he was aware he could not afford to slacken.

"Come Tom, we are nearly here," said Jambalee. He goaded Tom to continue. Suddenly, he stopped – pointing into the mist circling like a tornado in front of the grey mountain. "Look!" he said, and before Tom could work out what he was meant to be looking at, Jambalee was off again. "Come on!" he shouted as he bound forward, his little legs jumping up and down and stretching like a kangaroo as he began to run through the lush prairie of grey flowers.

Tom ran after his small companion, it dawned on him that he was being led toward the Circle of Life. As they passed over its border, a hazy grey mist swallowed the air as it rolled around, whizzing and hurling in a circular motion.

"You have now entered the Circle of Life – What do you wish from me, Son of Lindiarna?" bellowed a deep voice from nowhere.

"Lindiarna?" retorted Tom sharply "Who is that? I've never heard of Lindiarna! Who are you talking about?" Tom wailed. He was confused, but Jambalee was not. He gazed reassuringly into Tom's worried eyes.

"The Circle of Life will help us if we just agree to what it says," Jambalee encouraged, continuing to witness into Tom's eyes, trying to convince him not to worry and to remain calm.

****

The Shield of life, with the Sword of Strength and a Pouch of Magic

****

Chapter V

The McGuire Legacy

Tom stood still and quiet as a mouse, like a statue, wide-eyed and frozen in fear. He gazed watching the mystical, swirling, air, waft around him, whilst half listening to the Oracle. The Oracle roared, echoing his words, loud, and profound. They reverberated as he spoke,

"You have returned, to claim your throne, but you must cross Typheousina's wrath and the

Demonic around was deep in thought, oblivious to what the Oracle was saying to Jambalee. He began to think of how good Linda was at everything and how the voice – The Oracle – knew that he was a son from the mortal world. "Who was Lindiarna?" He wondered. He knew he had to persevere to find out. The turmoil whizzing around in his head was eating away at his thoughts. He realised that he was overwhelmed, embroiled in an environment that he had never seen or even ever associated with. He knew that someone, or something, thought he was the son of Lindiarna, who he had heard of when listening to Jambalee telling stories about King Cepheus, but he could not – did not – want to match the two to him. In Turmoil,

Tom was here for two reasons only; for the U-Targ and the safe return home to his Mum and family. As he tried to make sense of what this all meant. Jambalee lurched forward to the Circle of Life and slowly spoke.

"Your Oracleness," he began, nervously bowing forward in such a way that his ears flopped in front of is eyes, "we seek help and salvation from the great Typhoeusina." His voice broke in fear toward the end of his little speech.

Tom licked his lips and stared into the revolving, swirling mist. "Please, Oracle, you have to help the U-Targ, the Trolls."

After a short time, a voice charged from the swirling mist.

"Tom," I have watched you battle with Typhoeusina and your tussle with the branches of the Old Oak Tree. I know that you have walked many miles and climbed through the Mountains of the Moon." The Oracle and Tom formed a sudden silent pause. Jambalee looked at Tom and Tom returned his gaze. Tom's eyes weakened and became waterlogged as he suppressed his tears. Suddenly like a shot from the dark, a loud roar erupted from nowhere. The sky whizzed into a frenzy of colours and tweets, which sounded like birds hovering over the grey, misty sky. A whizzing tornado began to glow and as the sky turned into a pastel magnolia with cream and orange-coloured rosebuds, Tom felt that the Oracle had done something quite remarkable. He had answered Jambalee and Tom's request. It had to be, surely.

Tom was feeling quite emotional. He grabbed Jambalee's little hand, hoping that the Circle of Life had done what he thought it had.

"Has it just destroyed Typhoeusina? What's going on?" queried Tom anxiously.

Jambalee looked up at Tom's frightened face.

"Tom, I don't exactly know," he whispered. "Wait."

Suddenly, a voice came thundering and echoing through the air. – It was the Oracle once more, bellowing.

"I have set the U-Targ free and I have sent Typhoeusina to sleep. For how long will depend on how long it takes you to get back to your world!"

Tom frowned, turning Jambalee for assurance. The Oracle echoed once more.

"I have done this because you are the son of Lindiarna, daughter of Cepheus, the Great War Lord of Oblivionarna," howled the Oracle. The Oracle had spoken. The ground trembled and the dew from the trees fell in a myriad of shards to the ground.

"Great War Lord! Lindiarna!" Tom reiterated.

"Oh, Great Oracle-ness," snapped Tom when the tremors had ceased. "I do not know of Lindiarna. Who is this person?"

Jambalee tried to signal to Tom to be quiet, but it was too late – Tom had said what was on his mind. "You are young, Tom," he said.

"Have you forgotten how you battled with Typhoeusina? Have you not learnt anything from King Cepheus about how he won many moons previously? Did Jambalee not tell you?"

The Oracle's voice then roared once more.

"You must close your eyes and think of where you want to be," the Oracle bellowed.

"Lindiarna our True Queen "

Tom, gulped and sighed, He looked at Jambalee.

"Yes, who is this, what has it to do with me?" Tom persisted.

"Dear Tom, Lindiarna is YOUR MUM!"

There was complete silence. Tom, turned to Jambalee.

Jambalee looked at Tom and knowingly smiled.

The Oracle continued, "It is too dangerous for you both to go back the way you have arrived, as this bard is too great for you to learn."

Tom closed his eyes, slowly thinking of all that the Oracle had said and done. He had to be quick in focusing his mind to going back home. He thought of his Mum, and then he thought of his brother. His mind darted and flashed images of Mrs Morecraft, Mr Smith and Mr Jefferson, at speed. There were so many thoughts shooting through his mind.

"I have to be focused; I must think home! Think back to school," he muttered to himself.

After what felt like about ten minutes, Tom slowly opened his eyes. He had returned. He found himself in a dark place. There was a dank, damp ordure. He looked closely and found that he was back facing the door, which had led him into the exit point of boiler room. This is where Tom would renter the boiler room. He was sure to be back in the mortal world. He would meet up with James, to tell him about what he discovered. from where he first started his journey.

James, called out to his brother, Tom. I'm back," Tom echoed loud. He was jubilant at being so close to home. Suddenly, Jambalee appeared from nowhere.

"Tom, be aware, you have not returned to the mortal world, yet! Jambalee warned as his puddle-drop eyes became water logged. "You have helped us so much, in such a short time – the U-Targ, Daga and Pastureman, and Trolls have been set free from Typhoeusina's oppression." There was a sudden pause. Both Tom and Jambalee always found the time when Tom had to go home difficult. Tom knew he was going home, but he was worried for the U-Targ and the possible return of Typhoeusina. He hoped, though, that Jambalee and the U-Targ would be happy and much more secure. With the return of their homes. They could now live in peace.

Tom pondered about what the Oracle had said. He concluded that his Mum was connected to the land that he frequently visited. He also realised that Jambalee knew everything about his mother, but was for some reason had not said anything. It was evident that his mother, Linda, had some powers and it wasn't just a coincidence that the Oracle bellowed that he was the son of Lindiarna.

"Son of Lindiarna," an anguished Tom garbled to himself. "I wish it hadn't kept saying that. I must ask Mum about it" Tom confirmed to himself.

With that, he turned his attention to the door in front of him. He began to push open the iron door with all his might. As he did so, he wondered about his brother on the other side.

 "Oh Crikey, James," he chuckled. "I bet he's just been sitting there like some lame pleb!"

Sure enough, as the door opened and the hinges creaked, James was sitting on a bag of coal, drawing noughts and crosses, with some chalk he found – just as Tom imagined he would be.

James was using some broken chalk he had found on the concrete floor. Alone, he sat and played. As soon as Tom's arm appeared pushing the door wider, James jumped up in jubilation.

'You could have told me you were going for hours!' he moaned, relieved that Tom had arrived safely.

'Quick, we haven't got much time!' shouted Tom.

'Tom and James paced quickly through the boiler room past the water pipes, which looked like submarine tubes. They hurried back down the corridor up to Mr Jefferson's office. He saw both boys scurrying across the vestibule and stopped them.

Mr Jefferson was a large man, with a pot-belly and a suit that was way too small for him. E always carried a hankie in his hand. It was to wipe off his perspiration. Mr Jefferson was a very kind-hearted headmaster. He would always wear a three-piece suit and polished black shoes. He liked his food, which was evident as he was rather round in shape. Peering through his rimmed clear glasses, which always sat at the end of his nose, he summoned the boys.

'Ah, Tom and James McGuire! Are you two not going home? Or do you both have a detention?' Mr Jefferson looked rather puzzled as he peered through his silver-rimmed specs. Hearing no reply from the two boys, he continued. "Well? Since you both don't know what you are doing and where you are going, I will assign you some tasks. Follow me!" He instructed sternly. trying to throw his authority around.

Tom and James had guilt written all over their faces as they followed Mr Jefferson. He led the two boys up through the vestibule into the library then piled some heavy books onto their forearms, peering through his glasses, he could see how they buckled slightly with the weight of the books.

"Now, carry these down to Mrs Morecraft's class," he told them strictly. He face became ridged and tense.

"Yes, sir," said James subserviently, as they both carried the books to Mrs Morecraft's classroom. They marched through the corridor; James moaned at Tom.

"This is all because of you!" He shouted, squeezing his nose up at Tom.

Mrs Morecraft peered over the banister, smirking at both Tom and James, watching them both struggle to carry the books. Her face was crumpled up and creased in anger and rage, her evil green eyes prominent. She knew exactly what Tom had done and where he had been. But she who he was!

"I have been so worried about you; I wouldn't want anything to happen to you now, would I?" She said sarcastic smirk. She quickly swivelled, placing her contemptuous spindly cold fingers onto Tom's shoulders. Tom neck suddenly felt cold, as her green piercing eyes dazzled in a hypnotic trance.

Her malevolent voice had spoken. Her breath threw out flames and flickered like that of a dragon, so much so that even James shot his eyes wide open astonished in disbelief. Tom sighed with a sulk.

Carrying the books, James whispered,

"Drop her books and let's go home, because she is just weird."

Mrs Morecraft she was unearthly. It was her eyes, her hands, the way she spoke. Her whole demeanour.

Her drowned in disbelief that Tom had dared to battle with Typhoeusina and had still survived!

"Just like King Cepheus!" She blurted in rage.

Everyone gasped, locking their gaze with Mrs Morecraft.

"Yes... yes I am! Thank you for asking miss." replied an apologetic Tom. At that moment Tom realised there was a connection. He did not know how she knew about King Cepheus.

"What was all that about?" queried James. "Did we miss so much? Let's just get out of here, I've had enough."

Tom looked at Mrs Morecraft like some guilty puppy, ignoring James.

She peered with her sharp, glaring eyes and quickly snapped,

"Well, yes! We have started studying the story of Cepheus, but I know that you have studied that very well indeed already!"

Letting through a note of sarcasm as she spoke, Mrs Morecraft's voice angled with malicious intent towards Tom, as if to almost harm him. At that point, Tom knew he had to get home and that Mrs Morecraft and his Mum had some sort of connection in common. He sensed the uneasiness and atmosphere that was apparent. What did she know? Who was she? Why was she so cold a person and weird? Her cold look was frozen and her unearthly form shattered both Tom and James, draining them of all faith in good. They were shaken as Mr Jefferson ushered the boys out of the school. Mr Jefferson, the headmaster led the boys out to the front entrance. The school suddenly appeared so different. – it was empty and cold; deathly cold. The dark corridors spoke of an eerie silence. Tom had never felt such a spine-chilling coldness before.

"Phew," said James quietly, "What was that weird teacher on about?"

Tom looked at James, shook his head. "James "I don't know. C'mon," he said defiantly. "Let's go home."

****

Chapter VI

Lindiarna's Bard

Later that evening, Tom walked into the kitchen of his home, slowly sliding his body against the kitchen units.

'Don't clean the cupboards with your school shirt, Tom!' said his Mum annoyed at what Tom was doing. Linda frowned, and continued to prepare the evening meal. Tom looked at his mother, staring and not knowing if she was a real human, questioning himself and his dad and brother.

"Did you want something?" She asked.

Tom just smiled whilst leaning on the cupboard, before walking over to the fridge.

"We had a busy day today at school, Mum," he finally said pulling a drink out of the fridge.

"You, did? Oh good," she answered. Busy preparing the meal. She walked over to the cooker and placed the vegetables onto the stove. Linda knew Tom had been to Oblivionarna and had met up with Jambalee. However, she knew that she must not to tell Tom about her connection with the land as the time was not right. So, she continued to be oblivious to Tom's questioning.

"Mum, who is King Cepheus?"

At that point, Linda dropped the colander into the sink. She was facing the wall with her back to Tom. Her shoulders shuddered. There was an awkward silence; almost deathly. She turned slowly to her son. Leaning on the kitchen worktop, she stared right into his glowing, sharp eyes. Tom was hesitant and shocked at how his mother turned to face him. Completely mute, she took a deep breath and looked directly into his eyes.

"Tom," she said calmly, "I can't tell you yet, but I promise I will; but not just yet. You must trust me on this, please sweetheart." She held his cheeks in her hands, forming a cup. She dipped her eyes to resume her attention back to her cooking. Although, she realised Tom knew more than he should, at this moment and MAYBE, maybe MORKANN was back.

Tom looked at her. His Mum had confirmed in just one sentence that she knew everything and was not all as she seemed.

Tom walked up to his room. He was home and he was the son of Lindiarna. His mother confirmed his fear. His mind was awash with turbulence, with so many questions unanswered. "Who could he talk to? What was the link between his mother Mrs Morecraft? Who was she? Should he question his mother directly?" He wondered, in disarray.

It was clear; Linda did not want, or was not ready, to say. However, Tom knew his mother held all the secrets with all of the answers, but how was he to obtain those answers? When would she say? How would she say it?

His mind was thrown into disarray.

"I need to know, I must know," he thought to himself. This was the new challenge he now faced. He rummaged through his draws, frantically throwing out all his socks and his t-shirts, hoping he would find something telling him anything of who he was, or who his mother was. Tom could hear Lindiarna downstairs. She was normal; she didn't have three heads, fang teeth or purple hair. She was nothing like any of the characters in the books Tom would read.

He was really confused.

"Mrs Morecraft," he muttered to himself as he sat on the edge of his bed completely mystified. "What a name! She's always following me around, like some bad odour! James doesn't want to get involved – he is just tied up in his exams, and his work!" he continued to garble. "Oh James, will find out." Tom asserted.

At that point, a bemused and cautious Tom decided to walk downstairs.

****

Chapter VII

The Legitimate Cause

James was slumped on the sofa in the lounge. He had his legs stretched across all three seats. flicking over the television channels.

"What are you wasting your eyesight on - again?" asked an anxious Tom.

"Err... nothing really... just thinking about what happened today," James answered, playing with the remote control to the television.

Tom looked at James pensively, trying to map out in his head how to tell his brother the inevitable.

"James, yes! It was kind of weird, wasn't it?"

Replied Tom, pretending nothing happened out of the ordinary.

"Yes, I suppose it was. I waited ages for you.

There was a stifled silence.

"Tom. Where did you go after you went through the door?"

James had asked the question that Tom dreaded. He gazed at his older brother. He just took a deep breath in haling before he ate his lips.

"Yes, I did ask, you to join me, nevermind – next time."

"Ok, C'mon, let's eat,'" answered a calm James.

Both of the boys walked into the kitchen, where an anxious Mum awaited nervously. She knew that her boys, especially Tom, had discovered everything – and everything they shouldn't have found out. However, the time was not right and a lot had to be done first before they would able to confront Morkann.

The two boys sat down to eat deep in thought. There was an awkward silence that could be cut with a bread knife. It was razor sharp, and no one knew how to slice it. Tom's eyes fixed as he stared at the bread on the table. James began to munch on his stew with dumplings.

It was his favourite meal. James felt there was something that Tom saw in the tunnel he entered. He wondered how he would get Tom to tell him about his discovery.

Although the boys were together munching on their food, there was a deathly silence.

"You boys, did you have a good day?" asked a resilient Linda, trying desperately to maintain some normality at the table.

"Yes, mmm…it was just fine," replied James.

Tom quickly looked up and stared at James and then turned sharply at his Mum; would James say something about the boiler room? Would James tell his Mum what Tom had been up to?

"Can I go now to my room please, Mum?" Tom asked, his puppy eyes dropping into a pitiful glare. He knew this look always worked on his Mum.

"Are you finished?" Mum asked, staring at Tom, "Are you not hungry? Oh, well, if you really want to." residing to Tom wanting to leave his food. James, looked up. Linda, acknowledged him away from the table.

As Tom left the table, having not eaten much of the food, James stared at him. He felt that his behaviour was odd.

Mum?" James asked in a distinctly ruffled mumble.

"Yes?" replied Linda.

"Something happened today and it was strange." "What do you mean STRANGE?" queried Linda. She feared what James was about to state something that she did not want to hear.

Peering over his food, James looked his Mum straight in her eyes.

"Mum? Do you know Tom's been playing truant, and that he has been hiding?

"Well, don't tell me anymore". Snapped Linda.

"Mum, Tom has been sneaking off!" No, I...mean ... he has been going to a room... NO...great, how can I! How can I explain this? Erm... Mum?"

James tried desperately to get his words out, but they were all jumbled up. James, although normally articulate, was a nervous wreck.

Linda interrupted abruptly. She stretched out her arms and held James closely.

"James! Tell me, what is it? Tell me what happened today?"

Holding James by both his biceps, Linda demanded that James tell her what happened at school.

"James, I love you very much – both of you. Where did Tom go today?"

She was now becoming anxious and trying hard to control her emotions. James looked at his Mum and she released her grip from his arms. He looked straight into her eyes and gingerly, babbled, "Mum, something's going on Mum, and I don't know what it is." James, was incredulous.

"Don't worry James, I know." Linda answered reassuringly.

"I will speak to Tom, don't you worry."

Linda, kissed her son on his forehead. "You sleep tight.".

James was scared. At that point, James began to walk up to his room. When he got to the top of the stairs, Tom met him and led him to his room.

"Come here," he said conspiratorially. "I want to tell you something".

A puzzled James walked into Tom's room

"Tell me then!" he blurted.

His voice crackled and broke with anticipation.

Tom began to tell James of the events of the last four years at Prosperous High School, and that Mrs Morecraft was not who she said she was. Tom told James about what he had done and what he found out on his last visit to

Oblivionarna. Then Tom took a deep breath, turned around to look at a shocked James. James, was in complete astonishment. He was speechless. – Tom, continued and began to tell him about Jambalee, his new friend he encountered.

"So you see, that's the secret," he said finally. Both boys were very quiet, for neither of them knew what they should say. James looked at Tom and walked over to the long-standing mirror.

James, sighed. "Ermm, so, we Grandsons of a Warrior Lord? Huh. Beat that…" He turned to face his brother.

He squinted his eyes and squeezed his nose.

"Are you sure?" he questioned, flexing his muscles.

Tom smiled, got up from the bed and pushed James out of his room.

"I told you …yes!" retorted James.

****

Chapter VIII

The MorKann Link

The next day, both Tom and James got ready for school. Linda just watched pensively, thinking about what James had tried to tell her. When they arrived at the school, Tom and James felt different somehow. The Headmaster, Mr Jefferson was not present to greet them as he usually did. They continued to walk into school, there were no bikes in the bike shed, and there were no children playing in the playground.

"Are we early or something? Where is everyone?" James queried.

"No… No, I don't think so…" Tom answered hesitantly, as he quickly looked over his right shoulder and saw Mrs Morecraft waiting at the corridor to the boiler room.

"Yikes!" Look whose there.

"Why is she here?" Tom whispered to himself.

She was not dressed in her normal drab clothes. She had a spectral, creepy appearance; her Medusa hair was flowing – almost like Typhoeusina's heads! She held out her spiny hand and called for the boys to edge towards her.

"Come …come…". She enticed them to edge closer.

Her eerie slippery voice trickled through the corridor, bouncing off the walls. Her fingers were beckoning, pulling the boys closer. Her mesmerising eyes transfixed on one purpose. She was pure evil and her intent was not what it seemed.

"Oh crikey!" shouted James. "This is all your fault, Tom!" James became anxious.

"James, don't let her know that you're scared!" reasoned Tom.

"Scared? I'm petrified!"

"I just want to go to my lesson. I love Maths, I'll have you know!' James grumbled.

"Shush...shush! Do you feel something? I can't control what's happening? Why am I being

pulled? C'mon, let's go to her," suggested Tom.

Just as they were about to make their way forward, Their Mum, Lindiarna arrived at the school. She placed herself firmly in front of her boys.

"Mum!" Both James and Tom shouted in unison Although, surprised they were relieved to see their Mum. Whatever trance they had been in was killed off. The boys suddenly felt they had gained extra strength. They looked at their saviour; Their Linda was now going to save them.

"YOU! Lindiarna, why are you here?" squealed an angry Morkann, jolting with fury. Her spindly fingers melted when Linda raised her arm and began to suddenly levitate.

"Look!" gasped James, pointing at his mother.

"Wow! Go, Mum!" Tom was amazed.

"Morkann, why are you here? What are your intentions and why do you want to harm my boys?"

Linda hollowed.

Linda's boys were in total wonderment.

They watched silently as Linda interrogated Morkann.

"Morkann, who is she?" Tom wondered as he looked at James. Both of the boys were frightened as the rage and wrath intensified.

James tried to hide behind the bookshelves as his mother battled with her wit and celestial form to confront a vengeful Morkann.

Tom wished he could have Jambalee here with him to help – he would know what to do. Tom wasn't aware that Linda was still able to use her powers. King Cepheus had secured Linda's release into the mortal world by making sure she would not use the powers betrothed to her.

Tom had to find out who Morkann was – she knew of his Mum. Linda knew Morkann, so what was the story? He could see that there was friction, so much hatred. He had to find Jambalee to tell him more.

Tom slowly crept back into the corridor, whilst watching his mother and Morkann argue with their powers. James was aghast, shocked into what he was witnessing and feeling helpless. Tom had made up his mind – he had to get some help and James was not the right person to help him.

"Where are you going?" questioned James, watching intently. 'You can't go now!'

It was too late. Tom had entered the boiler room and was now heading towards the door. Everything looked so far away; distant, further than it done before. The door that would reach Jambalee seemed to have moved to the other side of the boiler room, but it hadn't.

This was Tom's mind playing games. The sweat trickled over his face and shoulders and he knew he had only moments to find

Jambalee. His mum was in danger, or was she? The door was found.

"Gosh, come, on... open...open," he moaned, as he tussled turning the door handle. Then he shoved at the old iron door – click, clank, cruck it was unlocked. He pushed harder and the door opened fully. Slowly and cautiously, Tom walked in.

The air was stale and crisp, icy cold. Darkness had fallen and there was a sense that all was not well.

Jambalee! Jambalee!' called out Tom, his voice reverberating in the callous cold air.

"Where are you?" Tom was worried; he was more scared than he had ever been.

"Tom, I'm here," answered a cold, shaky voice. It was Jambalee.

The character that had always just appeared, or popped up to see him, was now half his strength and extremely willowy, thin and fragile. His coat, which used to be tight and held together with one button, was now just hanging loose from his shoulders.

"Jambalee!" A shocked Tom uttered. "What happened to you? Was it Typhoeusina?"

Jambalee's frail little hands held Tom's as his quaint frame shook.

"No, it is not. You have to go back to your world".

"But I came to tell you," Tom interrupted,

"to ask you about Morkann."

Jambalee was visibly distressed. Tom wondered what had happened that would make his friend react in such a way. Tom's face sank with sadness. Jambalee, holding on to Tom, lurched over to him and dragged him to another part of Ripple Marsh. It was an arduous journey.

"Tom, it is Morkann who has done this. It is you – only you – who can save us."

Jambalee's head bowed and he collapsed near to Tom, who was even more befuddled and very frightened. Jambalee opened his pocket and gave Tom a magic white powder, which he had used in the battle with the Old Oak Tree.

"Here, I don't have much time," he said, passing the white magic powder contained in a casket to Tom. "Take this… you must use it to kill Morkann. Only then will you and Lindiarna be set free from her powers. Tom, the Shield of Life. I will give this to you again, but you must use it carefully and not in vain.'

Jambalee was clearly weak, unable to finish the rhyme. He looked at a tearful Tom.

"Your power has diminished, Jambalee. Why, tell me, what's going on?" Tom questioned.

Tom tried to help Jambalee walk and feed him some of the water from the drinking flask hanging from his coat. Jambalee lay down on the grey ground that was thick with brown moss. Jambalee waved his arm and groaned.

"Go! Go now if you want to save your mum and yourself. Go!"

He was adamant in his insistence that Tom should leave. So, Tom, armed with the Shield of Life, his sword and Jambalee's magic white powder, set off for the boiler room door. As he approached the corridor, he saw Morkann screeching and his Mum, flying gracefully and muttering words of Latin – or what sounded like Latin. These war words seemed apparently to keep Morkann at bay. When Tom saw Mrs Morecraft, now known as Morkann, he was completely astonished to see her appear as a malevolent Medusa-like figure.

She was evil and had changed her appearance to an abhorrent creature, with her penetrating cat's eyes sparkling and smart, bloodshot; her Medusa hair was swishing its serpents, hitting the ground. Her clothing was black and long and her silhouette figure grappled with the shadows. James had obviously fainted and now lay on the corridor floor, floppy and bedazzled.

Lindiarna appeared in a white robe, almost saintly, floating in radiance. There was a bright light around her as if her aura were present. Her face was pure and did not resemble Linda, the mother Tom knew so well. Her eyes and hair were soft and gave off a creamy, lustrous shine.

This was Lindiarna. Tom looked down at the shield he held in his hand – it was moving. The stones slowly began to lift in unison. They glistened as if they were telling Tom to go and protect his mother. Tom thought about Jambalee and how weak he had become and this was all due to Morkann. The vision of his weakened friend burning in his mind. He edged forward, knowing he had to save them.

****

Chapter IX

The Legacy Continues

Tom quickly ran to his Mum as he heard the rage that echoed around the school.

"YOU'RE back!"

"You are my worst enemy, I will kill you!"

"Vos es meus pessimus hostilis, EGO mos iuguolo vos!" Morkann squealed in Latin.

Her voice was bitter and stoic, as she howled like a banshee. "You thought that Moradiya would let you go and live in peace, you thought that just because King Cepheus had given YOU the power, you could live as you wanted! Ha ha…" She whined. Morkann was angry and Tom realised very quickly that she was a dark evil force out to get rid of his family.

Morkann, tossed her Medusa hair. She let it fall and drop. Screaming, "Oblivionarna does not need you, I am the Queen not you…Argh!" She lashed, as her battle began.

"Leave my boys alone Morkann! Your problem is with me!" roared Lindiarna.

Morkann, on hearing this, let her hair fall. Thin snakes wriggled onto her shoulders. Her black Medusa hair strands, twisted, ready to throw out, each tip with menacing leering snakeheads. Each one ready to spit out their tongues, trying to nip at who, whatever was near to them. Morkann, had shown her true form, as a Medusa like creature. In her rage she tried to take a swipe at Lindiarna and Tom. Tom dived onto the floor behind a chair, which was in the corridor. In doing so, the chair fell to the ground. Morkann screeched out a horrendous wail like a banshee.

Tom, held out his shield, pointing it into Morkann's face. The jewels began to lift and flicker into her eyes. Her green piercing eyes now, were wide, bloodshot and menacing. She shrieked even louder, wailing, fighting with the light shimmering from each jewel.

Lindiarna levitated over Morkann several times and each time Morkann would try and swat Lindiarna away, like a fly. Morkann wiped her eyes as Lindiarna looked sharply to James lying on the floor. She began to blow, creating a small mist to waft and confuse Morkann. The haze developed into heavy fog. Lindiarna, knew she had to try and hide James from Morkann's gaze, as he lay powerless on the cold slate floor.

Morkann turned and saw James lying on the floor, helpless. She had her chance. She glanced realising that Lindiarna was trying to hide James from her view. She was now after James! She knew Lindiarna would do anything to rescue her son. Morkann had to capture James if she was to succeed in her plot to oust Lindiarna.

Tom tried in vain to help his Mum and brother as he rushed to the other side of the corridor. In his pursuit, he knocked some vases to the ground. – They fell and rolled onto the floor. James stopped in his tracks and looked at them dancing on the ground, the ceramic teasing the concrete floor. Just for a moment he panicked. Tom ran past James lying on the ground.

Morkann, although initially pursuing Tom, glanced down at James, snarling and jeering.

"Go Tom, I don't need you anymore!" Morkann sneered.

Morkann now had James in her gaze and she was now after him.

Lindiarna rotated in the air and without apprehension, she dived to scoop James up

off the floor. Swish... it was too late –
Morkann had taken James. laughing and
wailing as she glided away. A distraught Tom
wondered what he could do next. He looked
at his Mum. He frowned, sad and melancholy.
Tom hurriedly pulled out the white magic
powder from his jacket pocket that Jambalee
had given him. He turned sharply to Morkann
and called out, his voice quivering in sheer
fright.

"Morkann!" he yelled, beckoning her. She
turned to him. She was shocked that Tom
dare call her. Tom locked his gaze at
Morkann peering down at the powder. He
held out in his hand that now shook. She
laughed hysterically and soared high up into
the air. She had scooped up James into her

arms, teasing Lindiarna and Tom. She was goading them towards her and eventually to fall into the evil trap that she had concocted. A worried Tom, unsure whether his idea would work, again yelled, "Morkann, wait! You will need this!" Holding out the small purple pouch containing the magic guiding powder.

"How else will you be able to stay in this mortal world?" Morkann shot, her glaring eyes drilling into Tom. She had stopped moving. Now hovering, if only for a second; but it was enough. Tom threw the magic powder over his shoulder, it shot into her face.

She screamed, dropping James instantly to the ground as she cried out, wailing like a banshee in pain. Her Medusa hair wafted while the tips of her hair branched out as small serpents. She was frenetically trying to wipe off the powder from her face her serpent-like hair, screeched, waving their demonic slithery tongues, to snap at the powder. Lindiarna seized hold of James and Tom. She flew out of the Georgian window on the second floor. Tom held the shield close as it shimmered in the dim light.

He began to try and make sense of what he had just done and what could have happened. He had been rescued and scooped up by his mum and saved from Morkann's clutches. James awoke, afraid and very confused. Their hearts were beating, purring and pounding fast, like a sports car engine with no sign of slowing down. Now that Mum had scraped up both the boys, she glided through the misty grey sky.

Lindiarna, was celestial, with her sultry silky golden hair and her soft pebble skin like lilies floating in a sapphire fountain. Her softly woven muslin cloth robe moved with the gentle breeze. The smog that Tom and James were used to seeing had vanished. Linda just smiled to herself, gently looking down on her innocent boys. She had scooped up her sons. They were the future of the realm. Carrying her boys, she asked them to be brave. She kissed Tom on his forehead as the wind caressed his hair. Linda, for that split second felt very proud.

Holding both boys, Lindiarna whispered, 'Tom, I must tell you about Cepheus, your Grandfather. Jambalee has taught you well!'

Tom was jubilant. He was now about to be let into a world that he had only seen glimpses of. He began to wonder about how his mother knew of Jambalee helping him – and how she knew about the boiler room, or did she know?

"Mum, I went back for the shield, do you know that?" asked Tom, curiously; elated that he was able to now relinquish his secret.

"Yes, I know everything," she replied softly.

"You mentioned you know about Jambalee? I saw him Mum, and he was so weak", said Tom, his eyes sad with concern for his friend.

Lindiarna knew everything that had happened and just nodded. In many ways she was relieved. Her sons were safe, even though Morkann had tried to pursue them she had made sure that Morkann could not harm her boys.

Gliding through the grey misty sky, the cold wind kissed Toms' face, He felt secure and reassured that Jambalee was indeed a good creature and that Morkann had to be defeated.

Tom understood at that moment that it was because of Morkann returning to her natural self – doing away with the façade of appearing as 'Mrs Morecraft' the teacher. He was able to see the real destruction she had caused. She had caused much misery and despair within the land of Oblivionarna.

"Tom, I know about the boiler room," said a calm Linda. Tom's mouth fell open in disbelief, as if he were catching flies. He was relieved that his Mum knew.

"Mum! You know?" he questioned.

Lindiarna smiled and gave him a sympathetic nod as the three of them landed in Tom's bedroom. James stretched out and gave his mum a big hug, having heard all of what Linda had said.

"I love you Mum," he said. 'I don't know about Tom's adventures, I don't think I can achieve what he has done but...", he broke off, starting to weep. Linda pulled him towards her and hugged him in a loving embrace. Tom was silent, reticent and shocked at what had just occurred. His Mum knew everything, but then all Mums generally do.

****

The lead **Centaur- Chiron**, in the battle of Typhoona. Battling with the evil Morkannis.

(This chapter includes Latin)

Chapter X

The Battle of Typhoona

The day of Hades had arrived. This was the day on which all in Moriadiya would abide by the spirits of the dead. The spirits had been kind to King Polyectes and he was about to repay them by initiating a battle with his rival, King Cepheus. It was a day on which King Polyectes would almost certainly win his battles. If the battle took place in

Moriadya, then the evil King Polyectes would almost certainly win.

The galaxy of Moriadiya had turned a hazy blue shade, with small red specks of dust floating in the atmosphere. Most of the ground was covered with pink sirens. The air was arctic and crisp and the rustling of orange, brazen-milled leaves cemented the tor.

"I shall wipe out Oblivionarna, Ego vadum deleo Oblivionarna is ero mei! It will be mine!" howled vengeful King Polylectes in Latin. This was the national language of Moriadiya. He swung his heavy-jewelled iron falcate sword high up in air.

He was a tall, large and very grumpy old King. He, judging by the lines on his face, must have been about a hundred and hundred and twenty years old! He had a beard as orange as a Satsuma, with a moustache to match. He was always miserable; this was because he could not defeat Typhoeusina. The most dangerous beast of all beasts and creatures to be found in the Magellanic galaxies. Polyectes knew it was only King Cepheus who could achieve the almost impossible. He defeated the serpent and freeing the Lupans, Daga, and all Trolls on Sky Mountain.

Today, King Polyectes wore a long grey robe, covered with metallic chains that swept the floor. It clattered as he stomped around the Palace in Moriadiya. He wore very large black leather boots and his face, which sometimes appeared through his facial hair, struggled to smile. His powder blue eyes were slanted and piercing, as if he were a wolf after its prey. Everyone who lived in Moriadiya was either frightened of him or of his presence.

His daughter, Morkann, was a Medusa figure – all wrinkly and creased up like an un-ironed shirt. She was the second daughter from his first wife, Queen Felicia. His first daughter, Princess Elyria, was imprisoned by Morkann as castigation for being too pretty!

King Polyectes' second wife, Queen Amy, who was from Oblivionarna, had a beautiful daughter who possessed a celestial singing voice and a soft, dewy complexion with a gentle temperament. She was named Princess

Annalisa, and was the fairest of the land, with sultry, dark eyes and burnished skin which emulated soft dusk dew like velvet silk.

However, Morkann rebelled against her and her mother for everything. She resented all that she did not have – her beauty, her singing talent, her clothes – absolutely everything! The fact that she was from Oblivionarna made Morkann even angrier. She desired just about everything that she did not possess. So Morkann had Annalisa, together with her mother, imprisoned in the towers of Bell à Noir, near the Clomp at Tumblewood.

The King was totally oblivious to what his daughter had done. Morkann, although she was fifteen years of age, blamed the serpent Typhoeusina for their disappearance. This perhaps was the reason why King Polyectes wanted desperately to kill the Serpent once and for all. It was only King Cepheus who knew where the princesses were placed and where Queen Amy would be found. King Cepheus tried to advise King Polyectes that he should not take his galaxy to war. Indeed, there was many an occasion when King Cepheus had stopped battles occurring and, if the truth be told, had even approached the court of Prytaneum.

This, of course, was the highest court in the Magellanic galaxies. King Cepheus wanted to stop the evil king raging war in a land that was now becoming barren and stricken with depravation. All of the beings and creatures were suffering, even the Lupans, the male Imps.

These were beings that resembled small fawns – half human and half rabbit – except instead of paws they possessed hooves. The female fawns were known as Dillyans and were very similar to their male counterparts, except they possessed silver wings and pink hair. Indeed, the only Imp to possess feet, as we know them, was their leader Jambalee. These were kept in black shoes with a bulbous toe.

On that day, Typhoeusina had been seen trying to break the clouds, with its heads slamming and crashing onto the ground. The cracks would appear in the blue plains, letting through the Lupans. The Lupans and Dillyans were small imps. They were able to speak both English and Latin and were extremely clever little creatures. They wore strange clothing. Their features were tiny, with small purple droplets for eyes and strange coloured hair, which generally popped out of a tattered black cap. Their coats, sometimes with a tail, were always made of green or brown tweed and the whole thing was held together by a single, brown old leather (or what looked like leather) button.

These little Lupans would scurry everywhere. They would move quickly, hovering and swaying to hide from Typhoeusina. Their leader, Jambalee, was a friend to King Cepheus and would always show an allegiance to Oblivionarna. He would also often play with the King's ten-year-old daughter, Lindiarna.

The battle commenced and the Wish Unicorn galloped through the land, telling the Lupans to hide and to gather all their belongings if they wished to save themselves. The Wish Unicorn was an elegant, magnificent creature with cloven hooves, together with a long, curved, solid, twisted silver horn that protruded precariously out of its forehead. He had an emerald-green fluffy tail, which would always swing through the horizon informing all, like a town crier, of what was about to occur.

This Unicorn was unique and extremely special, with its silver mane, curved horn and long, green fluffy tail. When this creature ran wild through the plains, all would then begin their slow journey across the galaxy into Oblivionarna to share among the U-Targ. These people, who lived in Oblivionarna, were colossal and had lived happily amongst all the life forms. They too feared Typhoeusina and Morkann.

The galaxy turned yellow in colour, similar to a medicinal syrup. This was going to be difficult and not without strife for both of the kings. King Polyectes summoned his legion.

"Meus proeliator, adveho, vos must iuguolo Serpent!"

"My warriors, come, you must kill the Serpent," he beckoned, speaking Latin in a tremendous deep voice.

The Morages all lined up in Tumblewood, holding their swords and petrus stones as each one knew only too well what would happen if they did not comply. King Polyectes glanced sharply over to his army of Morages. They were made up of lean, tall figures, brandishing their swords, bows and arrows and clad in red sulphur metallic clothing. Their faces were always stretched – motionless and taut. In battle, they would always walk in unison and were deadly to all that they approached. They would rapidly erupt into battle, without notice, with their fingers and hands which were long and slender like cats' claws waiting – ready for the kill. They were able to stretch their trim fingers like a praying mantis.

King Polyectes glanced once more at his army, shouting brusquely, "You must listen carefully, *Vos must audio dilgenter*! (Latin)"

He had not even finished his sentence, when suddenly a tumultuous roar came thundering through the air.

It was Typhoeusina, which appeared out of nowhere and was extremely angry. The deadly dragon swayed heads in fury. Their dazzling eyes as sharp as pins, as Typhoeusina's limbs wrestled with the terrain. It displayed its wrath.

Its heavy muscular heads bowed and trundled like an acrobatic dancer. Its eyes glared and gleamed, reflecting like a prism and glittering in the rays of the purple moonlight. The Morages suddenly began to turn and scuttle towards the Serpent, thrashing their swords furiously through the air, their deadly arrows flying through the trees in the hope that they would be able to attack the great Typhoeusina. But to no avail! This Serpent was too gigantic. The army's deadly arrows and swords tried to quickly bring down one of Typhoeusina's heads, but the Serpent had too many of them. The noise was shattering, and the trees and creatures that were in attendance suddenly turned into black soot.

King Polyectes looked on helplessly as he saw many of his evil Morages slain and defeated across the ground. The King rushed towards his army, trying to assist them, but what was before him was his army mortally wounded and scattered through the marshes.

He leapt from his horse and ploughed his face into the ground. He lurched as he dragged his body through the sludge of blood, mashed mud marshes and large ballistas and swords scattered across the plain.

(Latin) *"Typhoeusina, vos must sentio poena!"* "You must feel the Pain!" an angry King Polylectes roared in Latin. The King was incandesced with what he saw; his eyes and swell. He sweat gripped his face and began to swell with fury. He gradually looked up and witnessed Typhoeusina. The Serpent's dazzling eyes flashed, together with fumes of hell blowing through his snout, with flickers of light as he roared with a frenzied rant. It was imminent – King Polyectes would now be defeated and Typhoeusina would attack without haste.

Suddenly, the skies turned a turquoise-green colour. The grey clouds that remained hovered through the air, brushing it with soft strokes of wispy vapours. These were gliding fast, moving at a rapid speed. It was apparent that Jambalee, head of the Lupans, had summoned King Cepheus to aid the creatures of Moriadiya. He had realised that King Polyectes, although evil and a bad King, needed help. This was why the atmosphere had swiftly changed.

King Cepheus approached Ripple Marsh and trudged his way through the destruction that Typhoeusina had left behind in Moriadiya.

"Why are you here?" asked Polyectes, abruptly.

"I'm here to offer you help," replied a calm and collected Cepheus. "Do you want it?"

"You are not wanted here," growled King Polylectes. "Your land is in Oblivionarna!" (Latin) "Terra tua in Oblivionarna!"

"Why are you so afraid?" Questioned King Cepheus, in a spiritus prophecy manner.

Jambalee quickly popped up beside King Cepheus, appearing quite aloof and timorous. He was holding the 'Shield of Life'. King Polyectes looked down at King Cepheus as he stood holding his gallant sword and at Jambalee, who was clutching the shield. Its light, glistened leaping into Polyectes eyes, forcing him to raise his arm in protection. He shook his head slowly, trying desperately to avoid the dazzle from the shield.

King Cepheus was a kind King. He was tall, composed figure. His long, fiery-red hair was brushed back and neatly kept. His smile was radiant and his clothing emulated a blue flame. His eyes were grey and opaque, almost appearing like a pearl. There was a plethora of warmth with this King and Polyectes was extremely envious of him. Indeed, his child, Princess Lindiarna, who at the time was 10 years of age, was like any other – inquisitive, shy and very loveable. She had long, silky auburn hair and tantalising apple-green eyes. Her skin was dewy and soft, her lips were as red as a cherry and her hands were slender like porcelain.

King Polylectes did not wish Cepheus to become the Great War Lord; neither did he wish his child to succeed him.

"You will never defeat Typhoeusina!" Polyectes shouted as he grappled with the glare of the shield. "Go – and leave my land" – "*Vado Cepheus licentia meus terra , pro EGO iuguolo vos*!"(Latin translation)

King Cepheus moved slowly away. As he stood back both Jambalee and King Cepheus could see the great serpent roaring towards them. 'Look – we have to do something or we will all be wiped out!" argued Jambalee.

Typhoeusina was raging its war, and swiped one of his long double-edged fire flame tongues across to grasp hold of its prey – King Polyectes. The King was distinctly ruffled by its thud and size, and he hastily grabbed his ballista sword and waved it high up into the air at Typhoeusina. He quickly began to recite the verse of war: *"Vado vos mos abolesco! Vado vos mos abolesco!"* He hoped that the Serpent would vanish; but it did not. The King hurriedly slashed the air, in vain, struggling to get a hold of the Serpent's neck, torso, anything that would keep the beast at bay. It was all in vain.

Then out of the blue, King Cepheus appeared at his side. Along with Jambalee, they marched towards him, carrying the Shield of Life. Jambalee held the shield, making sure he was pointing it at Typhoeusina's obtruding, fiery, topaz eyes.

The shield dazzled, King Cepheus, raised his ballista sword, wielding it high. He threw the sword with all his might, managing to slash the throat of one of Typhoeusina's heads. It was the Shield of Life, which Jambalee carried bearing the jewels of the secret realm. The jewels in the shield dazzled. Almost lifting from it's case. The glare of each topaz and ruby stone reflected in a luminous radiance. Typhoeusina howled with fury – it screeched and its heads pounced, thumping, bumping onto the ground with a boom. It fell onto the soft sludge of the marshes.

King Polylectes, King Cepheus and Jambalee, held on to whatever they could as the earth quaked and shook. The bowing trees fell and moaned to the ground. Typheousina, the deadly dragon, was angry. It's heads floated up and down furiously from the lair. It dived to evade the dazzle of jewels iridescent from the shield. The shield shimmered causing a sharp prism into the Dragon's eyes. King Polyectes was forced to step back, glaring at the Serpent's anguish. It had finally been injured and it was King Cepheus who had carried out what would be the fatal blow.

Typhoeusina slowly howled and droned in pain. It had been harmed. It wriggled, slamming it's obstruse heads. Throwing it's short limbs, into the atmosphere. It was wailing, squirming and squishing. The serpent let out a piercing shriek. It lunged forward to expel its fire from its gullet and out of its mouth. It was covered in toothsome laser sharp teeth. Tom was mesmerised, crippled in fear, frozen his heart should explode. There was no point in trying to count how many teeth were present. There were just too many to count. It's ferocious flames of rage, spat out, like a volcano. It's triangular isosceles eyes blazed in a menacing glare. King Cepheus, had succeeded. The battle had been won. The King had defeated the great Typheousina.

King Polyectes would never be able to claim the throne as the Great War Lord. His evil plan had failed. All of Oblivionarna and Moriadya would now hail King Cepheus as their Great War Lord within the galaxies. It was only King Cepheus who had the courage and relentlessness to dare fight against Typhoeusina and win.

The Great War Lord, King Cepheus, knew that he would have to protect his daughter. Although he had won a ferocious battle with Typhoeusina. King Cepheus had been injured. His shoulder had been cut by the serpent's barbed tail. The King was nursed by the U-Targ, Daga and Lupans. They were all forever grateful for their lives being saved.

"You must be well, your majesty. The U-Targ spoke vehemently. "We are forever indebted to you. Typheousina, will return to its lair, and leave us alone now".

"We will be safe now and we can rebuild our lives".

Lindiarna, the beautiful princess.

The time had come for an ailing King Cepheus to hand down his reign to his daughter, Lindiarna.

Time had passed, but the battle of Typhoona would not been forgotten. King Polylectes was now an old man, too frail to pursue his reign in Moradiya. It was, the evil Morkann, who had stolen his throne cruelly, she had fooled her own father, because of greed and jealousy. Eventually, Morkann had used her demon Ghouls to oust her father, King Polylectes. Now, she wanted the ultimate prize! The demise of her arch enemy, Lindiarna. She was the true queen. This was role was bestowed by, the Great War Lord, King Cepheus, her loving father. He was a kind king, who had slayed the monstrous

Dragon, Typheousina. Linda was promised the throne, after the battle. Morkann, found the reason for her quest. She was now ready to oust all who stood in her way. Morkann wanted the crown, Linda would meet her demise. This would leave the evil Morkann to rule the galaxy and all the dominion lands!

All of Oblivionarna were extremely anxious as they awaited news of their King passing on the news of injuring Typheousina. Sky Mountain, thundered his pleasure that his King had won the battle. The throne was to be handed over to Lindiarna. She was now beautiful woman, and Morkann became more envious of everything Lindiarna stood for. The decision was taken after consulting the Oracle of Life and Lindiarna's friend and ally, Jambalee. It was decided that she would have to renounce Oblivionarna and all the creatures who resided there. She would have to live on Planet Earth as a mortal, away from the danger that was now around her. Morkann, the wicked ruler of Moradiya,was hungry for all that was nit hers. She was heartless and did not see any reason, why she should not rule the lands. All knew, the life of Lindiarna would be in danger. Lindiarna had no choice, she would have to be sent away, if she was to live. This was if there would be any chance of her, or indeed her offspring, returning to the throne. What all of Oblivionarna did not want was the wicked Morkann taking over their land.

Lindiarna was then granted permission to live, as a mortal on planet Earth. She would be safe away from the demonic wrath of Morkann, King Polylectes and their army of Ghouls, the Morkannis. This decision, although painful, was necessary and a heart-breaking step because King Polylectes and his wicked daughter, Morkann, would always seek revenge. The throne, to rule the planets was at stake. If Lindiarna was to return stability, to Oblivionarna and Moradiya, she would have to live. Lindiarna, she sent to live on Earth. It was important that no harm should come to Lindiarna. King Cepheus knew that if this happened, then Oblivionarna would almost certainly be ruled by the tyrant King Polylectes. This is what King Polylectes and his evil daughter Morkann wanted. The Lupans and Dillyans, together with all the other creatures, including the U-Targ, Daga and Pastureman on Sky Mountain, were already an impoverished life form. Living in Oblivionarna, they would surely all perish.

Jambalee suggested that Lindiarna wait until she had reached an age where she was able to cope with the mortals on their world.

As a consequence, "Linda" was invented. Jambalee had made arrangements for Linda to meet her suitor, Jed McGuire. He was to be the Father of Lindiarna's offspring. The worlds would unite and peace would live upon the planets.

****

****

Epilogue

McGuire & Morkann –The Revenge *vol.2*

Chapter I

It was a dark Sunday evening and it was raining heavily. The rain was banging and slamming at the windows with hailstones and thick droplets of water. Tom had his face pinned to the bedroom window as he peered outside.

"Gosh, look at this weather; it's so dark it's like looking into an abyss. These street lights just look like space ships," he moaned to his Mum. Linda was making his bed whilst Tom was busy breathing circles onto the window, turning it all frosty.

"Hmm... yes I wish you wouldn't do that.... Tom, can you please do something useful and not just stand there blowing onto the window?" Linda whined.

Tom turned around and looked at his Mum. "Tut, okay," he moaned. "Mum, can I ask something?"

"Of course, what would you like to ask?"

"Where did Mrs Morecraft...?"

There was a sudden silent pause. Linda froze. She looked at Tom whilst, still holding and shuffling the pillow, waiting for him to continue his sentence. "Do you mean Morkann?" Linda corrected sternly, looking down at her pillow, fluffing and sprucing the duvet.

"Yes. Where has she gone Mum?" asked Tom.

"Tom, you really are an inquisitive child. Listen, can you hear James playing the piano? It's lovely, isn't it?"

Linda, had changed the subject.

She didn't really to want to talk about Morkann. Tom realised quickly, how his Mum had changed the subject. Tom just looked intently at his Mum. He had to retrieve the answers that he so wanted to know, but how? In a quandary, he persisted.

"Tom, I need to talk to you. Come with me," Linda said, grasping Tom's hand as she led him of the room. "C'mon, Tom," she insisted. She was going to tell Tom about Morkann, as nervous as she was. Tom, in comparison, was extremely anxious. He followed his mum into her room.

"Close the door, Tom," said Linda, watching as her little inquisitive boy did as he was told. "You are a very good boy, and I know that you have learnt a lot of skills from Jambalee."

"You do know about Jambalee" Tom blurted surprised.

Tom was aghast, shocked as to how his Mum casually talked about an incredible creature, from a different planet.

Linda spoke softly, holding Tom's hands together as if he were praying. Looking into his soft gentle hazel eyes, Linda gently and calmly whispered, "This story begins long before you and James were here and I... well, I was a small child about the same age James."

Linda smiled to herself while combing Tom's auburn hair, and pushing his fringe back with her fingers. She appeared melancholy – her eyes became teary and she quickly let go of Tom and walked over to the tissue box. Drying her eyes, she sat down again and held Tom closely again.

"Tom, there is a King. A King, that wanted to always do the right thing. A King who would always take care of all his subjects, the people he loved, the animals, who would parade the Tor. He was strong and fearless, like you." Linda cupped Tom's chin and smiled to her little boy.

Tom was aghast, lost in bewilderment, his curiosity peeked. Staring at his Mum, with his wide grey open puppy dog eyes.

"The King, was your Grandfather!"

Tom, gawked at Linda, surprised his Mum, confirmed what Jambalee had already told him.

"Yes, I know that already Mum, Jambalee told me," Interrupted Tom eagerly.

"Yes, good, listen to the story," she said, smiling as she placed a kiss on his forehead.

"Your Grandfather was King Cepheus; was a Great War Lord and Morkann's father was the wicked King Polyectes. He was from Moraidiya. Did Jambalee tell you about him too?"

Linda gently pulled Tom away from her grasp. Her eyes dipped; she was looking to see Tom's expression and emotion on his face. Tom could hardly speak.

" Yes, I heard Jambalee talk about the Great War Lord, King Cepheus. He was very brave."

Linda nodded – it was rare for her to sit back and do nothing. Tom was surprised but happy that she had given him some of her time. Even though that was what Mums generally did. James had stopped playing the piano and walked into the room. There was a stillness in the atmosphere and it suddenly turned to an awkward silent. A pensive James quickly gazed over at Tom and then back to his Mum.

"OK, what's going on?"

"Oh, James, you always spoil things," complained Tom.

"Mum was about to tell me about the wicked King Polylectes and the evil Morkann. You interrupted and spoilt it all!". Tom grumbled.

"Just sit down, then!" replied Mum, smiling.

James took his place and Linda looked on calmly and smiled lovingly at her boys.

"Well, let me see now," continued Linda. "Moraidiya is a cold place – almost barren – and it's not too far away from the Mountains of the Moon, near the Sky Mountain. That's where YOU went right?" Linda asked Tom.

"Mountains of the Moon, Sky Mountain?" ruffled a bewildered James.

"Shush, James," answered Tom in frustration.

"Well, King Polylectes was always battling; battling for land, battling for who rules what and what rules who. It was awful," continued Linda. "One day, someone in the palace court, although we all think it was Morkann, suggested that King Polyectes invade another galaxy so that he would become more powerful and that he would then be able to overthrow the U-Targ, Daga, Trolls and, to top that Pastureman! – These were the beings who were denied so much. Tom, I think you have helped them so much." Informed Jambalee.

Tom, locked his hazel eyes with Jambalee in deep concentration. "Yes, I did. That was no easy feat! It was so dangerous, that multi-headed serpent was so scary. It was just so huge and it had so many heads. His eyes; I will never forget his eyes, Mum. If it wasn't for Jambalee." Tom cried, his words sounding as if was underwater!

Tom became quiet as he reminisced his terrifying encounter. Linda, smiled, endearingly pulling closer for strong hug Tom closer.

"Can someone just tell me who are all these people and creatures and things?" interrupted James.

"Shh, shush, James. In a moment."

"Let Mum finish please," commanded Tom, as Linda continued.

"Okay, eventually, King Polylectes decided to overthrow a land of the Magellanic Clouds – these were two irregular-shaped small galaxies, fused together to form a luminous patch in the atmosphere. One of those small galaxies was called Oblivionarna and the other Moriadiya."

"What are all these clouds, about? I didn't know you were into space," remarked James.

"Will you be quiet – please!" shouted Tom.

James was completely unaware of where Tom had been and what he had done and seen. He really was not one to get too worried very quickly, but this time as he glanced at his

Mum and Tom, both seemed scared and worried.

Linda was so composed – almost tranquil. She looked at both of her boys and smiled, knowing that they were absorbing the information very carefully. Tom was stunned; his eyes bright and wide open like a hooting owl. It all began to make sense and in his little head, he realised that there was more to this story than he had first discovered. Of course, James was completely astonished by all that he had seen and was now hearing. He was in a state of utter bewilderment.

Suddenly, a thunderous, tumultuous noise jolted at the window. It was like an earthquake had just occurred, but only affecting the one bedroom where all three of them were huddled together on the bed. The rain was ferocious and violent, pelting down like a tornado. The whole house shook and the lights began to flicker viciously – on and off at great speed. The pictures fell – one, two and three – shattering the glass onto the floor. There were splinters of glass everywhere; it glistened on the carpet, emulating spikes of diamonds. Linda took hold of her boys and threw the duvet over them.

"Quick, cover yourselves! And don't move – until I say so!" squealed Linda.

Linda had seen this entrance before and feared the worst; she was familiar with what was about to confront her.

"What's happening?" asked Tom from underneath the bed cover.

"Look!" yelled James, who had poked his head out to get a good look. He was pointing to a tall, svelte, black silhouette, sinking into a bright white light that was shining through the window. The street lamp shimmered its orange rays through the blustery curtains like lemonade fizz.

Linda slowly looked up in fear.

"MORKANN!' she whispered incredulously.

"How did you get back here?"

She stood still, and silent. Her statuesque shape did not flinch. Her Medusa-like hair was motionless. It was spirally as a spider's web. Morkann's eyes were smart and bloodshot, filled with rage and anger. Her face appeared taut and rigid and grappled to display her wrath. She was back and now wanted more than just REVENGE.

Tom peered over the fluffy duvet like a cowering lamb to the slaughter, but James hurriedly pulled him back.

"'The window, Mum. Look, it's moving!" James yelled. They all turned sharply in unison.

"NO!" Cried Linda.

****

If you want to know more about what happens to the family, we recommend you read the next book, from the series, The Adventures of Tom McGuire, vol.2- Morkann's Revenge –

****

I hope you enjoyed reading the book.

Comprehension time

Read the book to find the answers.

Quizzes & Puzzles

1) *How old is Tom?*

2) *How many siblings does Tom have?*

3) *How old is Tom's sibling?*

4) *How does Tom find Oblivionarna?*

5) *Who does Tom meet in Oblivionarna?*

6) *What is the first creature Tom meets in Oblivionarna?*

7) *Who does Tom fear at school?*

8) *What is the name of Tom's school?*

9) *How many boys are there in Tom's class?*

10) *Who does Tom wish to help in Oblivionarna?*

11) *How many siblings does Morkann have?*

12) *Where is Princess Annalisa held?*

13) *What kind of creature is Jambalee?*

14) *How many Queens are there in Moriadiya?*

15) *Why was King Polyectes miserable?*

16) *Who are the Morages?*

17) *What is kept at Clomp, Tumblewood?*

18) *Who is the Wish Unicorn?*

19) *Who is imprisoned at Bell à Noir?*

20) What are Lupans and Dillyans?

21) How many heads does the Serpent at Uroboros have?

22) What colour are Typhoeusina's eyes?

****

The Adventures of Tom McGuire – Puzzle

Please complete the crossword puzzle below

Across:

1. The War Lord of Moriadiya
3. Name of School
5. The Great War Lord
8. The friendly strange creature
10. A battle lost by King Polyectes
11. Daughter of King Cepheus

Down:

2. A troubled creature in Uroboros
4. The hundred headed serpent
6. Knowing all in the land
7. A rival character
8. Tom's brother
9. Mum
10. The main character
12. A place where adventure started
13. Name of History teacher

The Answers: -

The Adventures of Tom McGuire - Puzzle KEY

Please complete the crossword puzzle on next page.

Across:

1. The War Lord of Moraidiya (KING POLYECTES)
3. Name of School (PROSPEROUS HIGH)
5. The Great War Lord (KING CEPHEUS)
8. The friendly strange creature (JAMBALEE)
10. A battle lost by King Polylectes (TYPHOONA)
11. Daughter of King Cepheus (LINDIARNA)

Down:

2. A troubled creature in Uroboros (U-TARG)
4. The hundred headed serpent (TYPHOEUSINA)
6. Knowing all in the land (ORACLE)
7. A rival character (MORKANN)
8. Tom's brother (JAMES)
9. Mum (LINDA)
10. The main character (TOM MCGUIRE)
12. A place where adventure started (BOILER ROOM)
13. Name of History teacher (MRS MORECRAFT)

The Answers: -

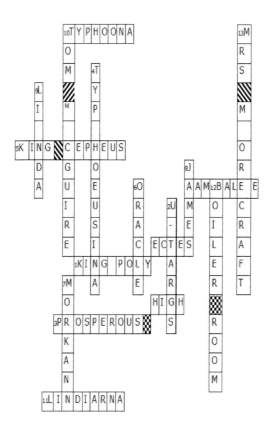

The End

Other Books in the Series: -

Morkann's Revenge - vol.2

The Dream Catcher

The Last Enchantment

Magnificent Reveal

Look out for 2nd edition for all books coming soon.

All books written are completely fictitious – any resemblance to any factual information is purely coincidental.

Please leave your review on Amazon co.uk.

I hope you enjoyed the book, look out for the Movie.

Glossary of Terms

This is to introduce you to the pronunciation and dictionary of words used in this book.

C
Cepheus – *King of Ethiopia. A constellation near the north celestial pole is named as Cepheus. (fact)*
Pronunciation: - *Sef-fee-ass (fiction)*
D **Dillyans** – *Female version of Imp type creature has pink hair and sliver transparent wings. (fiction)*
Pronunciation: **Dil-ye-ans**
J
Jambalee – *Leader of the Imps Oblivionarna. He is the only imp that*

O
Oblivionarna: - *one galaxy luminous patch on the southern sky, known to be an irregular shape. (fiction)*
Pronunciation: -   **obli-vi-arna**
P
Polycetes –*(based on factual character)*
In Greek mythology, Polydectes is who this character is based on. He wanted revenge so that he could marry his love. (fact)
Pronunciation: -   **poly-ec-tees**
Prytaneum –*In ancient Greek, a public hall of a Greek state or city, in which a sacred fire*

has feet. (fiction)	*was lit. This Court entertained successful foreign ambassadors. (fact)*
Pronunciation: Jam-bal-ee	**Pronunciation:- Pry-tan-e-um**
L	**T**
Lupans – *Imp type creature. They are the only ones that have hoofs for feet. (Fiction)*	**Typhoeusina:** *Derived from Greek word Typhoeus in Greek mythology. It is a monster with a hundred serpent heads, born to Tartarus and Gaia after the Titians defeated by Zeus. (fact)*
Pronunciation: Loo-pans	**Pronunciation: Tie-foo-sina**
	U
	Uroboros –*A circular symbol depicting a snake or less commonly a dragon.(fact)*
Lindiarna – *Princess of Oblivionarna*	**U-Targ** – *Scand avian mythology home of giants. (fact)*
Daughter of King Cepheus. (fiction)	**Pronunciation: You-targ**
Pronunciation: Lin-di-arn-a	
M	
Magellanic clouds – *Two diffuse luminous patches on the southern sky, now known to be irregular galaxies that are the closest to Earth. (fact)*	**g**

Pronunciation: - Mag-gel-lan-ic	
Morages – *Soldiers with allegiance to king Polyectes; only found in Moriadiya. (fiction)*	
Pronunciation: Mor–reg-es	
Moriadiya – *A name of an irregularly-shaped galaxy. (fiction)*	
Pronunciation: More–rad-di- a	
Morkann – *Tyrant wicked princess, Daughter of King Polyectes. (fiction)*	
Pronunciation: More-can	

The series has begun.

****

Printed in Great Britain
by Amazon